Bill Summers

FULL SUN PRESS

FULL SUN PRESS

Basking Ridge, New Jersey

CHAPTER 1

STAY WITH THE SWARM, OR RIDE THE WAVE?

S HANNON SWIFT KNEW THE CLOCK was running out.

Her head on her pillow, Shannon ran her eyes over the long crack on her ceiling. *I'm like my ceiling – cracking apart. How can something I love so much make me stress out like this?*

Two soccer teams wanted Shannon. She could choose only one. She loved playing for the Swarm, her town travel team. But now Shannon had an offer to join the Wave, the best under-thirteen academy team in New Jersey. She checked her watch: 3:17. She had less than three hours to decide.

Shannon closed her eyes and drifted off, but her phone rattled her. A text from Haley Punt, her best friend, next-door-neighbor, and Swarm teammate. *Wanna fire some shots at me?* Shannon smiled and tapped back, *Meet ya out back in five.* She bundled her long red hair in a ponytail and changed into her soccer gear. Hopping down the stairs two at a time, Shannon stepped out to the deck and grabbed a ball from the bin. A light mist dotted her face as she trotted onto the Square, the mini soccer field in her backyard. Shannon was eleven touches into a juggle when she heard the gate jiggle.

Haley walked in, but she wasn't alone. Behind her marched in every one of Shannon's teammates. At the back, Abby Rains and Montana West held a banner that read, *Swift and the Swarm – a Perfect Match.* Under the words, Abby had drawn a picture of Shannon in mid-air, cracking her favorite shot, a bicycle kick. The girls began to chant. "Shannon...*Swarm!* Shannon...*Swarm!*"

A lump rose in Shannon's throat. Haley wrapped an arm around her. "We love ya, Shan," she said. "You gotta stay."

Shannon blinked back a tear. The girls chose up sides and played a quick game on the damp grass. After it ended, Shannon watched the girls trail out through the gate. *I love those girls. How could I leave the Swarm?* Shannon flicked the ball up with her left foot and began another juggle. Out of the corner of her eye, she saw Haley coming back. The girls dropped into the grass. Shannon thumped a fist on her thigh. "I can't decide, Hale. It's driving me nuts."

Haley swept her black bangs off her forehead. "Shan, I got it figured out. Stay with the Swarm this spring, so we can win the State Cup. Then you can join the Wave."

Shannon frowned. "But Hale, the Wave may not want me then. This could be my only chance."

Haley yanked out a few blades of grass and tossed them into the breeze. "Shan, whatever you decide, I'll support you. As long as you stay on the Swarm."

Shannon snorted, and then the yard fell quiet. There was nothing more to say. For days, the only thing the girls had talked about was Shannon's decision – Swarm or Wave? Haley got up and started off. As she reached the gate, she turned. "My Dad's bringing home a new flavor tonight – Vanilla Key Lime Crunch. Come over after dinner."

"Maybe," Shannon murmured. It was the first time she hadn't jumped at the chance to try Mister Punt's homemade ice cream. Shannon tapped the ball toward her deck. She trudged up to her room, sat at her desk, grabbed a pen, and drew a line down the middle of her note pad. On one side she wrote her reasons to stay with the Swarm. On the other, she jotted why she should join the Wave. She counted, five to five. *I hate ties.* She stood and flopped on her bed. *I could flip a coin, but it would probably stand on its edge.*

Shannon picked up her pad and read her first reason to join the Wave – *get away from Chelsea.* Chelsea Mills, Shannon's enemy ever since she moved to Manchester, New Jersey, last summer. First, Chelsea tried to keep Shannon off the Swarm. When that didn't work, Chelsea and two other teammates quit the Swarm and joined their rival, the Monsoon. Then Chelsea injured Shannon in two games, and pushed her around in school. Shannon grabbed her pen and drew a red line through Chelsea's name. *If I join the Wave, I'll never have to play against that brat again.*

But then Shannon eyed the photos pinned

to her bulletin board. One showed Shannon and her teammates making a human pyramid in the backyard of the White House during a tournament in Washington D.C. Another photo showed Shannon and Haley lifting the trophy after that event. In a third shot, Shannon hugged her coach, Kate Wiffle. Shannon rolled over. *I love my teammates, love my coach. Love 'em more than I hate Chelsea.*

That night, Shannon sat for dinner with her parents and her older brother, Tim. An eerie quiet hung over the table. As Shannon cut into her bacon and cheddar quiche, she could feel six eyes on her. Finally, Tim broke the silence. "So Shan, you pick a team yet?"

Shannon took a deep breath and looked away from her mom. "I'm staying with the Swarm," she said.

Shannon's timing was perfect. Her mom nearly gagged on her water. "Shan, I'm surprised," Mrs. Swift said. "You sure?"

Shannon rolled her eyes. "I'm sure, Mom. I've nearly gone crazy over this."

Mrs. Swift held her stare on Shannon. "I

hope you're doing this for you, and not for your friends."

Shannon frowned. "Mom, I know you want me to join the Wave. But I can't do it."

Tim piled on. "Shan, the Wave is the best academy team in the country. You'd be nuts not to join them."

Shannon shot her brother a miffed look. "I love the Swarm, Tim. I'm not taking a chance with a new team."

"Sometimes you gotta take chances," Tim shot back. "If it was me, I'd join the Wave in a heartbeat."

Shannon squeezed her eyes shut. Her dad put a hand on her shoulder. "Shan, I think you made a good decision. I'm proud of how you thought it through."

"Thanks, Dad, but now comes the worst part. I gotta tell Coach Dash I'm not joining the Wave."

The room went quiet again. With half her quiche still on her plate, Shannon excused herself and plodded up to her room. She picked up Coach Dash's card from her desk. Her heart thumping, she tapped in his number. After the first ring, she poked, "end call."

Shannon bounced a palm off her forehead. *That was stupid, he'll know I called.* Her phone still in her hand, she paced across her white carpet, flicked up a tennis ball, and started to juggle. Her phone rang, and she saw *Jack Dash* on the screen. Shannon felt her hand shake. After four rings, she answered.

"Shannon, it's Coach Dash, sorry I missed your call."

Shannon tried to speak, but no words came out. Finally, she blurted, "Coach Dash, I'm so sorry, but I'm staying with the Swarm."

A few seconds of silence followed. At last, Coach Dash spoke. "I'm sorry to hear this, Shannon. I even had a number picked out for you."

Shannon felt a lump swell up in her throat. She didn't know what to say. "Shannon, are you there?" Coach Dash asked.

Shannon found her voice. "Coach, it was really hard. I just want to stay with my friends."

"I understand," he said. "Hey, the Swarm and the Wave both play in the Globetrotter Tournament in England this May. At least I'll get to see you then. Listen, I hope you have a great season with the Swarm."

"Thanks, Coach." Shannon hung up and flopped on her purple comforter. *Coach Dash sounds awesome. Maybe I blew it after all?*

Shannon's next call was much easier. She punched in Coach Wiffle's number, and she answered on the first ring. This time, the words flowed out. "Hey Coach, it's Shannon. I'm staying on the Swarm."

"Shannon, that's fantastic!" Coach blared. "I was so worried you might 'wave' goodbye."

"It was hard, Coach, but I can't leave you and my friends."

"You made my night, Shan," Coach said. "And guess what? I'm going to make you the captain of the Swarm."

Shannon's jaw dropped. "But I'm still pretty new. Plus, last fall we had different captains for each game."

"You've earned this honor, Shan," Coach replied. "You always put your teammates first. The girls look up to you. I'll tell them at our first indoor practice. We can meet for lunch before then, go over what I expect from you."

Shannon ended the call and clicked off. Wearing her first smile of the day, she tapped a quick text to Haley. *Staying on the Swarm.* The response came fast. *Hooray!*

Later that night, Shannon took her phone to bed. She went online and searched, 'captain.' *Leader of a sports team.* Shannon smiled. *It's cool that Coach wants me to be captain, hope I can do a good job.* She shut off her light. For the first time in a week, she slept through the night.

Two mornings later, Shannon was spreading strawberry jam on her toast when she heard the newspaper go 'thump' on the porch. She went out and picked up the *Manchester Mirror*. A chilly breeze nudged her back inside. She sat at the kitchen table and opened the sports section. The headline jumped out at her.

CHELSEA MILLS PICKED FOR THE WAVE SOCCER TEAM

CHAPTER 2

CAPTAIN SHANNON, ANGRY OLGA

SHANNON FELT HER HEART POUND. She read the story. *Manchester's Chelsea Mills has been chosen to play for the Wave, an academy soccer team for under-thirteen girls. Last fall, Mills was the leading scorer in the Morris Hills travel league, with fifteen goals. "Chelsea is a tremendous player and a natural scorer," said Jack Dash, Wave coach. "She was an easy pick and we're thrilled to have her."*

Shannon sneered. *Easy pick? I was your first choice!* She stared at the picture of Chelsea, smiling out at her. *That's the first time I've ever seen her teeth.* Shannon tore out the picture, crumpled it up, and stuck it in the trash bin. She was mad, and she was mad for being mad. *Why am I reacting like this? I should be happy. I don't have to play against that bully any more.*

But Shannon knew why she was steamed. Chelsea had moved up to a better team, a team that Shannon could have joined. *Now people will think Chelsea is better than me. No way is that girl better than me!* Shannon got up and began to pace across the black and white tiles on the kitchen floor. *Maybe Mom and Tim were right, maybe I shoulda joined the Wave.*

On the following Saturday morning, Shannon was juggling her tennis ball when she got a text from Coach Wiffle. *Shan, lots to talk about... Captain Swift and Chelsea Mills. Meet at the Coffee Shop at noon?* Shannon smiled and tapped back, *See you there.*

A few hours later, thick gray clouds hung low as Shannon set out on the three-block walk into town. She tried not to nibble her lip, but her teeth ignored her. *I'm excited to be captain, but nervous too. I mean, do I really deserve this, when every other girl has been on the Swarm longer than I have?*

The first snow of winter began to fall. A

stiff wind pushed big wet flakes sideways into Shannon's face. She pulled her pale blue scarf over her nose and walked faster. Climbing the steps to the Manchester Coffee Shop, Shannon passed a man on a ladder, hanging a string of holiday lights around the window. Shannon stepped in and spotted Coach Wiffle's bright yellow Swarm ball cap, her blond ponytail poking out the back. Shannon walked over. Coach stood and they hugged.

"Great to see you, Shan. I'm so glad you decided to stay."

"Me too, and now I don't have to play against Chelsea."

Coach nodded. They sat in facing seats. Shannon ordered grapefruit juice and a blueberry muffin, Coach asked for a sausage and cheddar omelet. Coach leaned in. "Okay, tell me how this sounds...Shannon Swift, Swarm captain."

Shannon nibbled her lip. "I'm not sure, Coach. What if other girls want to be captain?"

Coach sipped her water. "Like I said, Shan, you've earned it." She took out a sheet of paper and put it in front of Shannon. Shannon eyed the word at the top of the sheet – ACRONYM. "Coach, that first word, I can't even say it."

Coach chuckled. An English teacher at Manchester High School, she loved words. "ACK-ROW-NIM," Coach said. "It's a way to shorten a series of words. You take the first letter of each word in the phrase. You put them together and bingo – you have an acronym."

Shannon nodded, but Coach could tell she was lost. "Here's an example, Shan. When people want something done right away, they say, 'ASAP.' That's an acronym for, 'As soon as possible.'"

Shannon's eyes lit up. "Aha, now I get it."

Coach sipped her water. "Now look at the acronym on your list."

Shannon eyed 'CARE.' Coach went on. "That describes the four qualities I look for in a captain. C is for cool. That means you stay calm, no matter what crazy stuff happens around you."

"I can do that," Shannon said.

"It will be harder this year," Coach warned. "Last fall, you were the new girl. You took everyone by surprise. Now everybody knows you. Every team is going to be on you, like white on rice."

Shannon squinted. "White on rice?"

"It's a saying," Coach explained. "White rice is white all over. You're gonna be covered, like rice is covered by white."

Shannon rolled her eyes. "Okay, so, what does the 'A' stand for?"

"A is for attitude. Shan, you know why your teammates like you? You're upbeat. You're confident. You have fun. When you show those qualities, your teammates will follow your lead."

"We have a good team, so there's no reason to be negative," Shannon said.

"But we just moved up to the top flight in New Jersey," Coach countered. "That means we'll play better teams. You need to stay positive, even if we lose."

"Got it, so what about the 'R'?"

"It stands for respect," Coach said. "Shan, you must respect everyone – yourself, your teammates, your coach, your opponents, and the referees."

"Okay, and the 'E?'" Shannon asked.

Coach Wiffle put up a hand. "Slow down,

we're not done with respect. As captain, you must make sure that every teammate shows respect." Coach stabbed a piece of her omelet. "We have one player who likes to scold her teammates when they make a mistake."

Shannon leaned in. "You mean, Olga?"

Coach nodded. "When she does that, you need to stand up to her."

"But Olga's been on the team much longer than I have."

"Doesn't matter, you're the captain."

Shannon squirmed. "Olga has a nickname, you know. The girls call her 'ogre.' If I yell at her, you know she'll dish it back."

"Don't worry," Coach said, "I'll back you up."

Coach put her finger on the E. "That stands for effort. Give your best, every practice, every match, every minute. When you do that, you'll inspire your teammates to do the same."

Shannon gobbled the last bite of her muffin. The waiter left the check. As Coach dug through her wallet, Shannon heard the door swing open. She looked up and saw a familiar figure walk in. Suddenly, that muffin was doing somersaults in her belly. Chelsea Mills strutted up to the table.

She wore a bright red jacket. On the crest was a large blue wave, over the words, *New Jersey Wave*. Chelsea nodded at Coach and Coach nodded back, no words spoken. Chelsea faced Shannon. "My jacket's pretty cool, huh?"

"Nice colors," Shannon answered.

Chelsea grinned. "I had my first practice with the Wave yesterday. It's an awesome team."

"I'm sure it is," Shannon said.

"So, I was checking out our schedule," Chelsea said. "The Swarm and the Wave are playing in the Globetrotter tournament in England. Who knows, we might play each other."

"Bet it would be a great game," Shannon replied.

"Yeah, great for the Wave," Chelsea sniped.

Coach Wiffle put money on the table and stood. Shannon rose in a flash. She turned to face Chelsea. "Merry Christmas, Chelsea." Chelsea just stared. Shannon followed Coach out the door. On the sidewalk, Coach patted her shoulder. "Shan, you just had your first test as captain, and you aced it. Chelsea tried to get under your skin, but you kept your cool."

Shannon smiled. A bit later she started for home, her boots squishing the fluffy layer of snow on the sidewalk. *I'm captain of the Swarm, pretty cool. No way I'd be captain of the Wave.*

As she reached Orchard Way, Shannon saw Haley playing in the snow with her poodle, Alfie. The snow had turned Alfie's black fur white. "Hale, I barely recognize Alfie," Shannon called out. Haley ran over. "I think Alfie's cuter with white fur. I might have to bleach it."

Shannon snorted. Haley asked, "You coming back from town?"

"Yep, I just met with Coach Wiffle. Get this, Hale. She's gonna make me captain."

Haley broke into a grin. "Shan, that's great! You deserve it."

"Thanks. By the way, Coach told me not to tell anyone."

"You mean, besides me? Don't worry, my lips are zipped."

Shannon nibbled *her* lip. "Hale, you think everyone will be okay with me being captain?"

Haley tossed her head back. "Come on, you know Olga. She'll throw a fit that'll bounce off all eight planets."

Shannon frowned. Haley swept an open

palm through the air. "Don't sweat Olga, Shan. Coach will keep a lid on her."

A few days later, Shannon's mom drove her to the Swarm's first winter practice. It was a quiet ride, and Shannon knew why. "I know you wanted me to join the Wave."

"That's behind us, Shan," Mrs. Swift said. "You're going to have a great season on the Swarm."

Shannon nodded. *Nice of Mom to say that. Wonder if she believes it?*

Mrs. Swift dropped Shannon at the gym at Manchester Middle School. Stepping inside, she heard her stomach growl. *How will the girls react when Coach says I'm captain?* A bit later the girls gathered around Coach Wiffle. "We have an exciting season ahead of us," Coach said. "We move up to a tougher league. And in May, we go to England for the Globetrotter tournament."

"England, baby!" yelled out Abby Rains.

Coach smiled. "I'm happy to share some news. Our captain for the spring season is Shannon Swift."

Most of the girls cheered, but not all. Shannon

stole a look at Olga. Her cheeks were red, her lips curled shut. She opened them. "Coach, don't we pick captains for every game?" Olga asked.

"We used to, but Shannon has earned the role," Coach said.

"She's been on the Swarm for a few months," Olga shot back. "What about the girls who have been on the team for four years?"

Shannon felt a chill grip the back of her neck. Coach set her eyes on Olga. "Look, we have lots of players who could be good captains. But Shannon is our leader on the field. It makes sense to have her as our leader off the field."

Olga didn't back down. "Why don't you let the players pick the captain?"

"We'd all pick Shannon," Haley shot in.

"No we wouldn't," Olga fired back.

Chatter rumbled through the huddle. Coach put up her hands. "Girls, Shannon is our captain, that's it. Now follow her on a few laps around the gym."

Shannon broke into a trot, the girls close behind. Haley ran up beside Shannon. "I told ya, Shan."

Shannon nodded. "Olga is really ticked."

"Yeah, and you know why," Haley went on. "If she was captain, she'd think she could boss us around."

Shannon trapped a laugh in her throat. After a few laps, Coach asked Shannon to lead the girls through some stretches. As Shannon worked through her routine, her eyes kept landing on Olga. *Wow, that scowl is etched on her face.*

And that's how it went, for the next three weeks. Olga showed up to practice wearing the same pout. She hardly ever talked to Shannon, or anyone else. The only time Olga spoke was to call out someone's mistake, or to blame someone for *her* mistake. Each time Olga erupted, Coach would tell her to stop. But this was one habit Olga couldn't snap.

At the last indoor practice, Coach asked Shannon to stick around. "Shan, we need to talk about Olga. At practice, I can deal with her. But once the season starts, it'll be different. If she yells at a player for the wrong reason, you have to confront her."

"What do you mean, 'the wrong reason?'" Shannon asked.

Coach went on. "If Olga scolds a player for lack of hustle or a mental mistake, that's okay.

But if she yells at a player for a physical error, we can't accept that. No player who shoots over the bar needs to be told she screwed up. Got it?"

Shannon sighed. "It won't be easy, she'll yell right back."

"Like I told you, I'll handle that," Coach said.

Shannon nodded, and she and Coach walked out of the gym. On the ride home, Shannon thought about her new role. *I like being captain, except the Olga part. I mean, will I be able to stand up to her?*

As the spring season neared, Shannon felt better about her decision to stay on the Swarm. Chelsea had transferred to a private school, so Shannon never saw her. But the weekend before the Swarm's first game in April, a headline in the *Manchester Mirror* stirred her juices.

MILLS LEADS WAVE TO TITLE IN FLORIDA

Shannon read the first sentence. *Manchester resident Chelsea Mills scored three goals in three games to lead the Wave, the under-thirteen academy team, to the championship of an international soccer tournament held in Miami this weekend.*

Shannon tore out the story, balled it up, and stuffed it in the waste bin. *So Chelsea scored three goals in Florida. Big deal, I'll score three goals in our first game, then she can read about me.*

CHAPTER 3

THREE GOALS, TWO ACHY LEGS

S HANNON WOKE EARLY ON SATURDAY, her dream still fresh in her mind. She had dribbled a soccer ball across the country, tapped it through corn fields, up and down mountains, and across deserts. Sitting up, she saw her comforter in a heap on the floor. *I kicked my comforter off the bed, guess I made it to California.*

Shannon rolled up her window shade. Small white clouds hung like wads of cotton under a blue sky. *Perfect day for our first game.* Shannon swung out of bed, her eyes drawn to the tennis ball on her carpet. She flicked it up and began to juggle with her feet and thighs. On her tenth touch, the ball caromed off her foot and hit the carpet. *Ten with a tennis ball, not bad.*

Shannon stepped into her yellow slippers and bounded down the stairs. She turned into the kitchen, where her dad stood over a frying pan. "Fired up for your first game, Shan?" he asked.

"Can't wait, Dad. I'm tired of reading about Chelsea, now she can read about me."

Mr. Swift shoveled the first blueberry pancake onto a plate. "You need to forget about Chelsea Mills, Shan."

"How can I when she's all over the newspaper?" Shannon replied. "She scored three goals in some tournament. You know my answer to that? I'm gonna score three goals in my first game."

Mr. Swift slid three pancakes in front of Shannon. "Don't worry about scoring. Just play your game, and the goals will come."

Shannon cut her pancakes into twelve pieces and poured out a pool of cinnamon syrup. She jabbed a piece and dragged it through the pool. *Dad's right, but I still gotta get three goals today.*

Two hours later, Shannon was the first player to put cleats on the grass at Freedom Park.

Once all her teammates had arrived, she led them on a warm-up lap around the chalk. As Shannon reached the last corner, she looked over her shoulder and saw Olga, bumbling along at the back. Shannon shook her head. *That girl is gonna be trouble, I know it.*

After her last stretch, Shannon jogged out to meet the ref and the captain of the Flame. Shannon lost the toss. The Swarm would play the first half against a mighty wind whipping in their faces. One minute into the match, a Flame midfielder dribbled down the flank and launched a high cross. Haley stepped toward the ball but the wind kicked up, pushing it over her head. She backpedalled and leaped, but the ball sailed over her hands and ducked under the bar. Flame 1, Swarm 0.

Haley hung her head. Olga jogged over. "Come on, Haley, you knew the wind would take that ball!"

Shannon heard Olga. She trotted over to Haley and patted her shoulder. "Forget about that one, Hale. Now you know to stay back, be cautious."

"Thanks, Shan," Haley said.

Then Shannon ran over to Olga. "You can't yell at Haley, Olga, she was trying her best."

Olga glared. "She blew it, big time."

Shannon felt her heart thump. "Yelling at her is not going to help, Olga. You want to encourage her, make her feel good about the next one."

Olga shook her head. Shannon gritted her teeth and jogged off.

As the game wore on, the wind was like an extra player for the Flame. Late in the half, a Flame defender smashed a long, high ball toward the box. Olga misjudged the ball's flight. She headed it backward, right into the path of a Flame forward. The girl ran on and lashed a rocket into the far corner.

Shannon jogged to Olga. "Don't worry, Olga, it happens to all of us. We'll get it back." Olga looked at Shannon. "Thanks," she muttered.

At halftime, the Swarm jogged off buried in a 2-0 hole. In the stands, Mrs. Swift tapped her toes on the cement. "They're in big trouble now."

Tim waved a hand. "Cut the drama, Mom. They got the wind in the second half. They'll blow the Flame out."

The Swarm gathered on their bench, Coach Wiffle pacing in front of them. "Keep your chins up, girls. The wind will be our friend in the second half." Coach swung her eyes to Shannon. "We're gonna try something different," Coach went on. "Shannon will move up top, play on the left side. Let's play balls down that flank. Shannon can use her speed to own that space, spray balls into the box."

Shannon eyed the captain's band on her left sleeve. "Girls, we've rallied before. We can do it again." Shannon scanned the faces of her teammates, pausing at Olga's smirk. "Olga, you're playing great, keep it up." Olga's smirk faded, and Shannon smiled to herself.

Five minutes into the second half, Shannon fed Abby in the circle and bolted down the flank. Abby chipped a high ball toward the corner. Shannon raced past two defenders and gathered the rolling ball at the corner of the box. The keeper charged out. Shannon cocked her leg, drawing the keeper into a slide. But then Shannon slowed her leg and dinked the ball wide of her grounded foe. Dinked it a little too hard. As the ball rolled near the end line, Shannon took a peek at her narrow angle. She swept the inside of her boot into the ball. Falling to the grass, she watched the ball kiss the far post and tumble across the line. Shannon got up and darted over to Abby. "Great ball, Ab!"

Ten minutes later, Montana swiped a pass in the circle. Shannon took off, and Montana spooned a high feed toward the corner. As Shannon collected the ball, three opponents fenced her in. Her eyes up, she spotted Abby darting free toward the far post. Shannon lofted a high cross into Abby's path. Abby ran on and stuck her head into the ball. It arced over the keeper and bounced into the far corner. Swarm 2, Flame 2.

Abby ran over and leaped into Shannon's arms. "Sweet pass, Shan!" she yelled. In the stands, Tim turned to his mom. "Okay, Mom, who's in big trouble now?"

Now the Swarm could taste victory. They attacked in waves, forcing the Flame keeper to make a series of athletic saves. When the Swarm won a corner kick, Shannon and Abby looked at each other. Shannon tapped her right ear, signaling that she would prowl at the far post.

As Abby lined up to take the corner kick, Shannon ran from the penalty spot toward the near post. She paused, and then she darted back toward the far post. Abby's kick was coming down ten yards off the goal line, but Shannon figured the wind would carry it closer to the goal. She edged inside her foe, jumped, and snapped her forehead into the ball. It flew over the keeper's hands and poked the net in the far corner. Swarm 3, Flame 2.

Shannon shook her fists. *That's two.* She looked at her dad on the sideline. He held up three fingers. Shannon nodded. *Three minutes to get my third goal.* The Flame pushed players forward, trying to even the score. Their left wing crossed into the box, but Olga stepped into a clean volley that sailed all the way to the circle.

Now the race was on, and Shannon was not going to lose. She beat two defenders to the rolling ball and broke in alone against the keeper. When the keeper strayed far off her line, Shannon chipped the ball over her head. As it flew toward the bar, she crouched. *Get down, ball, get down!* The ball nicked the bottom of the bar and brushed the net. Shannon's teammates buried her under a pile. A minute later the ref blew her final whistle. The Swarm had a 4-2 win, and Shannon had her three goals.

Coach called the Swarm in. "Girls, my word for the day is, 'METTLE.' It means showing courage when you're up against a wall. We got behind, but you didn't panic. You showed your mettle, that's why we won."

The huddle broke. Shannon turned away, but Coach grabbed her arm. "Great game, Shan. And I saw you stand up to Olga after their first goal. Now you know why I made you captain."

Shannon smiled. "Thanks, Coach." Too tired to say more, Shannon grabbed her bag and walked over to her family. "Super game, Shan," Mrs. Swift raved. "How does it feel to score a hat trick?"

"Great," Shannon replied as she gave Tim a high-five. "But the four-goal rally feels even better."

"That was some comeback," Mr. Swift added. "I was worried at halftime, but you outran them in the second half."

"Yeah, my calves ache, first time ever."

That night, the Swifts put on a movie. After a few minutes, Shannon nodded off. When the movie ended, her mom woke her. Shannon looked at the blank screen. "Wow, guess that movie was a real snoozer."

"We had to turn up the volume," her mom said. "Never heard you snore like that."

Tim nodded. "It sounded like a jumbo jet was landing on the roof."

Shannon laughed. But then she yawned. "I'm beat, going to bed."

Trudging up the stairs, Shannon could feel her calf muscles twitch. *This is weird. Maybe I'm not in such good shape after all.* Five minutes later, she was back in full snore.

When Shannon woke the next morning, she pulled up the league website on her computer. Checking the scoring leaders, she saw that she was the only player to rack up three goals in the first game. As Shannon scanned the other names on the list, it hit her. *I'm not going to see Chelsea's name on here. Wonder if she'll still send me those crazy emails.*

Seconds later her phone beeped, an email. *Bet that's Chelsea.* She read. *Shannon, I just read about your hat trick. Great job, keep it up! – Coach*

Dash. Shannon smiled. *Wow, I didn't join the Wave, but Coach Dash still follows me. Pretty cool.*

Shannon put on her yellow slippers and went down to the kitchen. Tim was pouring syrup over a stack of French toast, and Mr. Swift had his nose buried in the newspaper. "Shan, this is some story about your game," her dad said. "Listen to this comment from the Flame's coach. *'Shannon Swift was too much for us. She ran hard the entire match. We just couldn't stay with her.'*"

Shannon broke into a grin. "Let Chelsea read that."

But Tim had a warning. "Every coach in the league will read that, Shan. You're gonna get smothered, just like my French toast is smothered in syrup."

Shannon eyed her brother. "Bring it on, I'm ready."

CHAPTER 4
DOUBLE VISION

In English class that Friday, Shannon drifted into a daydream. She was swinging her boot into a bicycle kick when she thought she heard her name. Startled, she sat up. "Uh, sorry Miss Peters, could you repeat the question?"

Giggles bounced off the walls. Miss Peters walked back to Shannon's desk. "I asked if I was boring you, Shannon. I think you just answered my question." More giggles. Shannon felt her face heating up. She wanted to crawl under her desk. *Wow, I got soccer on the brain, better snap out of it.*

The next day, Shannon woke to sunlight spilling onto her comforter. She pulled back her shade and gazed onto the Square. *Perfect day to play.* Shannon sprang out of bed, flicked up her tennis ball, and bashed it into her wall. *I feel another hat trick coming on.*

Two hours later, Shannon was warming up at Freedom Park when she noticed two girls on the Rockets. Twins. Tall, both with long black ponytails, and both staring at Shannon. Shannon stared back, but the girls didn't look away. *That's weird.*

Shannon won the coin toss. At noon on the nose, she started the match by tapping the ball to Abby and dashing out wide. She turned to look for a pass, but the twins had put the clamps on her. Shannon darted back across the field, her finger pointing in front of her. Abby tried to feed her, but one of the twins cut in and bashed the ball high and far.

The girl sneered at Shannon. "Number eleven, you're not gonna touch the ball." Shannon ignored her, but the girl was right. After five minutes, Shannon had touched the ball only once – on the kickoff.

In the stands, Tim turned to his mom. "Shannon must be seeing double by now."

Mrs. Swift nodded. "Yeah, but she's working

hard to get open. Her teammates need to get her the ball."

A bit later Olga cushioned a cross on her thigh and dribbled out of her box. Shannon sprinted into free space on the flank, and Olga rewarded her with the ball. Shannon looked up and saw the twins bearing down. "Go, Ab!" she yelled.

Shannon swung her leg back. When both twins jumped, Shannon tapped the ball under them and burst ahead. Another opponent closed in. Shannon cut left, but the girl stuck out a boot and chopped her down. The ref called a foul. Shannon rose, needles of pain stabbing her hip. *Whoa, that was a nasty tackle.* She hobbled for a few seconds before regaining her stride.

As the half wore on, Shannon tried to break free with short, slanting runs. But each time a teammate tried to feed her, a twin broke up the pass. When yet another pass got thumped away, Shannon felt her patience running out. *If my teammates can't get me the ball, I gotta steal it.*

A minute later a Rocket back tried to feed her wing, but Shannon lunged and got a boot on the ball. She dribbled toward the box, her foe fast on her heels. As Shannon wound up to shoot, the back slid in and clipped her down. The ref whistled a foul, but Shannon wanted more. "Come on, ref, I got hacked from behind," she wailed. "That should be a card!"

The ref glared. "Zip it, eleven, or I'll stick a card on you."

Shannon bit her lip. She jogged toward the box while Montana lined up the kick. As Shannon took her spot, she felt a shoulder thump her back. "You got nothin', eleven," sassed one of the twins. Shannon turned to face the girl, just as Montana delivered her kick. The ball sailed over Shannon, and the other twin headed it clear.

"Stay in the game, Shan!" called out Coach Wiffle. Shannon put up a hand. *Lost my cool, can't let that happen again.* When the first half ended, Shannon had touched the ball only six times, and she'd drawn five fouls. As the girls huddled by the bench, Coach Wiffle paced. "They're draped on Shannon like a wet blanket," Coach said. "That means we have an open player, sometimes two. Come on, girls, move the ball, and move off your passes."

After the huddle broke, Coach pulled Shannon aside. "Keep running hard, Shan.

Those twins are getting tired, we'll catch 'em flatfooted." Shannon nodded.

In the second half, Shannon ran like a hunted deer. But each time she got the ball, the twins quickly penned her in. Shannon passed well out of traffic, but her teammates failed to find the frame. As the game wound down, neither team could sniff the goal. When the Rockets' keeper snagged a cross, Shannon looked to the sideline, saw her dad hold up one finger. *Gotta do it now.* The keeper launched a high punt that Olga headed out wide. Shannon beat the twins to it. Seeing Montana flash up the flank, she lofted the ball toward the flag. Montana gathered on the run, and Shannon bolted for the box. One twin grabbed her shirt, but Shannon swatted the arm off. Montana thumped a cross. Shannon studied the ball, curling in behind her. *Okay, time to get on my bicycle.*

Crossing the eighteen, Shannon turned her back toward goal and leaped. She swung her left leg up and lashed her right boot at the ball. *Thwack!* It was a clean strike. As Shannon thudded to the grass, she turned and saw the ball arch over the keeper's hands. *Get down, ball!* Shannon whispered.

Thunk! The ball banged the bar and bounced into the goalmouth. An alert Montana had raced in. She got to the ball first, but spooned it over the bar. "Montana!" Olga screamed. Shannon sprang up and darted over to Olga. "Don't yell at her, Olga."

Olga locked eyes with Shannon. "She just blew an easy goal, Shannon."

"Yeah, and she doesn't need you to remind her."

Shannon jogged to Montana. "Forget about it, Mon, you'll get the next one."

But there was no next one. The game ended scoreless. The Swarm gathered by the bench. Coach Wiffle swept her gaze across each face, saw only frowns. "Girls, my word for the day is 'IMPROVISE,'" Coach said. "It means that when things aren't going our way, we have to adjust." Coach paced, her eyes on the grass. "Look, Shannon is getting double-teamed, even triple-teamed. You have to keep your head up, find open teammates."

Olga threw up her hands. "We're trying, Coach."

"We need to try harder," Coach shot back.

When Shannon reached her family, her

despair poured out. "That was crazy! The whole game, I felt trapped in a cage." She pushed down her socks, studied the nicks and cuts dotting her ankles and legs. "Plus, I got raked every time I got the ball."

Tim spoke. "The ref must've called them for ten fouls against you."

"Yeah, and he missed the other twenty," Shannon ranted.

"Shan, you didn't get many shots today," her mom popped off.

Shannon tossed her head back. "I know, Mom, you can't remember the last time I didn't score. I tried, ya know."

Mr. Swift struck a positive note. "Shan, that was some bicycle kick. I thought it was going in."

"Thanks, Dad, I hit it good, just not good enough."

"Montana really blew that rebound," Tim cracked.

"That's great, Tim, you sound like Olga," Shannon snapped. "But you're right. It's like no one on our team can shoot, or get me the ball."

Tim looked at her. "Like I said, Shan, you got

a bull's eye on your back. Every team is gonna bottle you up, and twist the cap shut."

Shannon said nothing. Later that day, she sprawled on her bed and thought about the game. *Maybe I got double-teamed because the other team had twins. Maybe it won't happen again.*

But it did. The following Saturday, the Magic boxed Shannon in with two players, sometimes three. She ran hard and got her share of the ball, but she had little room to maneuver. Her passing was sharp, but her teammates failed to mount a potent attack.

Late in the match, Shannon made some long, gallant runs with the ball. But each time she got near the box, she got fouled or lost the ball in a thicket of legs. In the final minute, a Magic player scored off a scramble. The Swarm lost, 1-0.

After the game, Coach Wiffle paced in front of the huddle. "We're still not running off our passes," she griped. "Remember, make a pass, and then make yourself a target. That's how we keep the ball moving and create chances to score." Shannon looked at the captain's arm band on her sleeve. *I should say something, but I have nothing good to say.*

After the huddle broke, Shannon walked over to meet her family. The ride home was quiet. When Mr. Swift pulled into the driveway, Shannon got out and headed for the backyard. "Where are you going?" her dad asked.

"Gotta work on my moves. I lost the ball, like, four times."

Mr. Swift shot her a sideways look. "Shan, you had three players on you. Plus, you just ran hard for eighty minutes. Come in, let's have lunch."

Shannon kept going. She grabbed a ball from the bin on the deck, walked to the edge of the Square, and dribbled hard to the other end. Nine more times she pushed the ball across the Square. After a short rest, she blasted ten shots with each foot. Sweat rolling into her eyes, Shannon climbed on the trampoline and smashed six bicycle kicks into the netting. She wanted to run a few sprints, but began to feel woozy. Instead, she picked up the ball and plodded toward the house. *I'll do my sprints in the morning, after I finish my three-mile run.*

The next morning, Shannon woke an hour later than usual. She rolled over and dozed for another forty-five minutes. Fighting off a yawn, she got up and put on her running gear. As she entered the kitchen, her dad looked up from the paper. "Morning, Shan. How about an omelet?"

"Gonna run first," Shannon said.

Mr. Swift put down the paper. "Not a good idea, Shan. Your legs need to recover."

"I got tired in the second half, that's bad."

Mr. Swift took off his glasses. "Of course you got tired, you galloped like a gazelle for eighty minutes."

"I'm getting double and triple-teamed, Dad. To get open, I have to be able to outrun everyone."

Shannon dropped to the carpet and began to stretch. Her dad spoke. "This is against my better judgment, but I'll let you run on one condition," he said. "Keep it short and slow."

"I will."

Her stretches finished, Shannon tapped a text to Haley. *Going for a jog – wanna come?* Haley answered, *You crazy? I got tired watching you run yesterday.*

Shannon snickered at that. But then Haley sent another text. *Okay, I'll keep you company, as long as you go slow!* Shannon thumbed back: *Deal, see you by the mailbox.*

Five minutes later, the girls met. "One mile, right, Shan?" Haley asked.

"We'll run to the end of the cul de sac and walk back," Shannon said.

"That's a mile and a half," Haley said, a hint of protest in her voice. "I'll do it, as long as we run at my pace."

Haley stepped into a slow trot. The girls ran side by side for a hundred yards, but Shannon had had enough. "Hale, I feel like I'm walking."

"I feel like I'm sprinting," Haley huffed. "Remember, Shan, I'm a keeper."

They trotted on, until Shannon couldn't take it anymore.

"I'm takin' off, Hale. I'll catch you on the way back."

"Deal," Haley said.

Shannon shifted gears, her stride growing longer. Soon, she had left Haley four mailboxes behind. As Shannon made the turn in the cul de sac, she looked up the road. She could see Haley, already jogging back toward their houses. Shannon pushed herself harder. Three mailboxes from home, she caught Haley. "Come on, Hale, race ya to my mailbox."

"You win, Shan."

Shannon burst into a sprint. She shot past her mailbox and flopped into the grass. A minute later Haley joined her. "Shan, that was not an easy run."

"Hale, I gotta go hard, it's the only way I know."

"You're scarin' me, girl."

"You saw what happened in the game, Hale. I hardly got the ball."

Haley finally caught her breath. "This run was good for one thing, Shan. It reminds me of why I play keeper."

Shannon laughed at that. A bit later, Haley made the short walk home. As Shannon headed for the house, she pumped a fist. *I bet no other girl in our league ran this morning.*

After practice on Tuesday, Coach Wiffle called the girls in. She dug into her backpack and pulled out a folder. "Our trip to England is getting closer. You know what that means, it's project time. By the time we get there, we'll be experts on England and its capital city, London."

Abby groaned. "Coach, we know about England already. It's old, it rains all the time, and they drive on the wrong side of the road."

The girls howled, but Coach scowled. "Make fun of England all you want, Abby. Just remember, if not for England, you wouldn't be playing soccer."

Abby crinkled her nose. "Say what?"

Coach went on. "Soccer was invented in England in the eleventh century. Whole villages would play against each other. They would play across hills and streams until one team got the ball into the center of the other team's village."

"That's crazy," Shannon said.

"Wait 'til you hear what they used for a ball," Coach said. "Try a pig's bladder, or the skull of a dead animal."

"No way," Abby shot in. "They'd break their foot."

Coach wagged a finger. "Back then, players could use any part of the body, hands included."

Shannon shook her head. *How weird is that?* Coach held up a stack of papers. "On each sheet I've written something about England, along with a clue. I want you to write a story on your subject, three hundred words, and make sure you write about the clue. Questions?"

"Three hundred words, that's a big number, Coach," Abby cracked.

The girls roared, and Coach went on. "Here's the best part. I spoke with your social studies teachers, Missus Peck and Mister Bloomer. They both agreed to include the paper you write on England as one of your three class papers for the spring term."

Coach opened the folder. "Okay, when I call your name, come up and grab your sheet." Shannon was called first. Her sheet read: *Trafalgar Square. Clue: pigeons.*

Abby was next. *Big Ben. Clue: coins.*

Haley followed. *Food. Clue: bangers and mash; bubbles and squeak; toad in the hole.* Coach gave every player an assignment. "I want you to dig deep," she said. "Visit the library. Poke around on the Internet. Before we go, we'll share what we learned."

"So, Coach, what's your assignment?" Abby asked. Coach shot her a playful look. "I'll tell you about cool words that have different meanings in England than they do here. Plus, I'll have a few surprises up my sleeve."

As the girls headed for their bags, Shannon walked over to Coach. "Coach, what's a Trafalgar Square?"

Coach smiled. "There's only one, Shan. Look it up, read about the pigeons. You'll be shocked at what happened to those poor birds."

When Shannon got home from school on Wednesday, she hopped up to her room and checked her workout schedule. *Three miles.* She changed into her running gear, stretched on her carpet, and bounced downstairs. Stepping out the front door, she was met by calm air and a clear sky. Shannon set her watch and stepped into a jog. *This time, I gotta beat twenty-four minutes.*

Shannon chugged along. As she neared the green mailbox a mile from her house, her watch read 8:10. *Too slow!* She picked up her pace, made the turn in the cul de sac, and headed back. Drawing even with the green mailbox, she saw 16:30 on her watch. *Yikes, only seven and a half minutes to finish my last mile.* Shannon pushed harder. Reaching the bend fifty yards from her house, she eyed the number on her wrist. 23:50. Shannon burst into a full sprint. She flew past her mailbox, and saw 23:59. "Yes!" Shannon called out, pumping a fist toward the sky.

Shannon dropped into the grass and basked in the warm sun. A minute later Haley rode up on her bike. "Shan, you run again?"

"Yup, best time ever."

"Hey, my dad's bringing home a new flavor tonight, Coffee Oreo Crumble."

"Sorry, Hale, I'm layin' off ice cream for a bit."

Haley's mouth fell open. "Shan, you run into a tree?"

Shannon snorted. "Have a scoop for me."

"Don't worry, I will," Haley said as she pedaled off.

Shannon got up and plodded to the garage. She grabbed a bottle of water from the fridge and guzzled it in one tilt. *Okay, time for some sprints.* Shannon stepped into the backyard, where she dashed across the Square eight times. For another ten minutes, she dribbled and shot. Her shirt soaked through, she went inside and sank into the thick carpet in her family room. *My legs feel tired, so I must be getting stronger.*

On Thursday, Shannon practiced with the Swarm. She was planning to take Friday off, but then she saw the sports section in the *Manchester Mirror*. A big story about the Wave, winning another national tournament. Chelsea Mills had scored seven goals in four games. A photo showed Chelsea sprinting up the field, waving a finger in the air.

Shannon stuffed the paper in the trash bin. *What a showboat that girl is.* She hustled upstairs, changed, and stretched. Her adrenaline pumping, Shannon hustled outside and stepped into another run. This time, she finished three miles in 23:52, her best time by seven seconds.

Shannon walked to the garage, pulled a water bottle from the fridge, and took a long drink. *I'm in the best shape of my life. Can't wait for tomorrow.*

CHAPTER 5

BAD SHADE OF RED

AT DINNER THAT NIGHT, SHANNON'S fork felt heavy. She stabbed at a pea but missed. At last she speared it, on her third try.

"Shan what's on your mind?" her dad asked.

Dad always knows. "I'm nervous about tomorrow's game. I can't let my teammates down again."

Mrs. Swift pushed her eyebrows up. "You haven't let anyone down."

"We haven't scored in two games, Mom. That's on me."

Tim waved that off. "Shan, that's crazy. You work harder than anybody."

Mr. Swift eyed Shannon. "Speaking of hard work, did I see you finishing a jog this afternoon?"

"A short one."

"Why are you running the day before a game?" her dad asked.

"Cuz I gotta be able to outrun the whole other team."

"You're not a machine, Shan," Tim shot in. "You gotta let your legs rest."

"My legs are fine," Shannon retorted. "I'll prove it tomorrow." She stuck her fork in a crouton, and it broke in half.

After dinner Shannon went on her computer and searched, 'Trafalgar Square Pigeons.' She opened a story and began to read. Her eyes flared with anger. Jotting notes on her pad, she filled two pages. In the margins, she wrote her reactions. *Unfair. Cruel. Bring back the birds!*

Her busy day catching up with her, Shannon rested her head on her desk. An hour later, she woke to a tap on her shoulder. "You fell asleep in your chair, Shan," her mom said. "Time to turn in."

Shannon took two steps and slipped into bed. Mrs. Swift pulled the comforter over Shannon's shoulders. Still in her T-shirt and shorts, Shannon slept through the night.

At Freedom Park the next day, Coach Wiffle sprang a surprise. Olga and Shannon would switch positions. Shannon would play center back, Olga would move up to center mid. "I want Shannon to sneak up into the attack," Coach explained.

Olga scratched her cleats on the grass. "Why is it always about Shannon?" she griped. "I mean, I haven't played midfield in years."

"We're in a rut, Olga," Coach answered. "We need to shake things up."

"But we've never played this formation," Olga whined. "It's a big risk."

"Sometimes you need to take risks," Coach shot back.

Five minutes into the game, Abby latched onto a loose ball and led Montana down the flank. Sensing a chance, Shannon dashed out of the circle toward the box. Montana crossed, and a Cheetah rose up and snapped into a powerful header. The ball flew out of the box, right into Shannon's path. As three Cheetahs closed in, Shannon swung her boot into the ball. It caromed off a defender's shin and rolled softly into the keeper's hands. Cheetah center back Stella Razer glared at Shannon. "You're so overrated, girl," she sassed.

Shannon glared back. "Yeah, and you got a big mouth."

Shannon jogged away. *That was dumb. Don't waste your energy running your mouth.*

Minutes later Shannon pounced on a loose ball in the circle. Spying Abby darting up the flank, she floated the ball toward the corner. Abby collected on the run and Shannon broke for the box. Abby crossed, and Stella volleyed the ball out, right at Shannon.

Shannon cushioned the bouncing ball on her thigh. As it fell to her foot, she sensed a pack of Cheetahs on the prowl. Her head up, Shannon saw Abby cutting in from the flank. She threaded a low ball between two Cheetahs. It rolled into Abby's path, ten yards from goal. Abby ran on and fired, but the ball sailed two feet over the bar.

Shannon threw up her hands. "Come on, Abby!" she wailed.

Abby shot Shannon a puzzled look. Shannon put up a hand. "Sorry, Ab." Shannon tapped her head. *That was a physical error. Keep your mouth shut!*

Later in the half, Shannon cut off a pass near the top of her box. Seeing open space, she surged ahead. But as she neared the circle, she pushed the ball a bit too far. Stella Razer raced up and made a clean tackle, her cleats scraping Shannon's ankle on her follow-through. "Aah!" Shannon yelled as she tumbled to the turf.

The ref waved play on. With Shannon down, Stella had a clear path toward goal. She dribbled to the top of the arc and lashed a low dart that knuckled over Haley's hands and snuck inside the far post. Cheetahs 1, Swarm 0.

Shannon got up and glared at the ref. "I got fouled!" she yelled.

"She got the ball first!" the ref fired back.

In the stands, Mrs. Swift turned to Tim. "Shannon never talks on the field. Today, she's yapping at everyone."

"Yeah, she's really frustrated," Tim replied. "Hope she doesn't boil over."

Shannon limped off the field. Coach Wiffle handed her an ice pack. Shannon dropped on the bench and stuck the pack on her ankle. Minutes later, the Swarm jogged off at halftime, down 1-0. Coach Wiffle turned to Shannon. "Come here," she said.

Shannon got up and hobbled over. Coach frowned. "You're too hurt to play, sit down."

"No way, Coach, I'm going back in."

"No you're not," Coach shot back. "You're done for the day." Shannon pitched her water bottle into the grass and slumped on the bench.

With ten minutes left in the game, the Cheetahs scored again. Shannon got up and tested her ankle. She approached Coach. "I'm fine, you gotta let me play."

Coach looked into Shannon's eyes. "Let me see you run."

Shannon took five quick strides, turned, and ran back. "How much pain do you feel?" Coach asked.

"None," Shannon fibbed.

Coach put Shannon in at midfield. As she ran back on, the Cheetahs' coach yelled, "Number eleven is back on, girls." Shannon bit her lip. *I'm gonna get boxed in again.*

The Swarm couldn't get the ball to Shannon, so she decided to get it herself. Running like she had a motor on her back, she chased the orb all over the pitch. Three times she tracked down loose balls, but each time she got fenced in. Once she lost the ball on the dribble, and another time she played it too far ahead of Abby. The third time, she cracked a long shot that sailed over the bar. That's when Stella Razer jogged up. "You should change your name to 'Shannon Slowpoke,'" Stella razzed.

"Get outta my face," Shannon snapped back.

With time running out, Shannon jockeyed for position under a goal kick. She jumped, but her sore ankle kept her just a few inches off the grass. The ball flew over her and came down on Stella's boot. Stella took off, and Shannon gave chase. *That girl got my ankle, time for some payback.* As Stella burst up the field, Shannon slid from behind. She was a whisker late. She caught Stella's ankles, chopping her chin-first to the turf. The ref blew her whistle. "Number eleven, get over here!" she shouted.

Shannon saw the anger on the ref's face. *Oh no, I might get a yellow.* The ref took out her book and held a card over Shannon's head. A red card.

Shannon's mouth fell open. "Red card?"

"You led with your cleats," the ref said. "Now get off the field." Shannon dragged her feet toward the sidelines. Olga ran over. "That was really dumb, Shannon, now we have no chance."

Shannon glared at Olga. She started to speak, but swallowed her words. In the stands, Mrs. Swift turned to Tim. "I knew she should have joined the Wave." This time, Tim said nothing.

The Swarm lost, 2-0. After the final whistle, Coach Wiffle called the girls in. As Shannon joined the huddle, she could feel eyes burning through her. Coach started to speak, but the Cheetahs broke into a loud chant. "Cheetahs, Cheetahs!"

"What bad sports," Olga snapped. Coach waited until the chant ended. "My word for the day is 'KNACKERED,'" she told the girls. "In England, it means, 'worn out.' We're all tired. Take Tuesday off, we'll practice on Thursday only, and we'll be fresh for our game on Saturday."

The huddle broke. Shannon fought back tears as she walked to her bag. Coach Wiffle's hand landed on her shoulder. "Stay here." When the other girls were out of earshot, Coach leveled her eyes on Shannon's. "That was a reckless foul, not what I expect from my captain."

"I got frustrated," Shannon said.

"We all get frustrated," Coach shot back. "It's how we deal with it that counts."

Shannon started to walk off, but Coach cuffed her arm. "I heard you yell at Abby after she shot over the bar."

"It was stupid, I won't do it again." Shannon twisted her cleats into the ground. "I feel like I'm letting the team down. I don't get the ball, I don't score. We're losing."

"You're getting marked out of every game," Coach said. "The girls have to learn how to make things happen without you."

Shannon walked off, Coach's words rattling in her head. *Make things happen without me?* Shannon swung her foot through the grass. *Coach is nuts.*

Shannon met her family at the car. "Tough game," Mr. Swift said.

"Yeah, and I don't want to talk about it." Shannon stuck in her ear buds for the ride home.

An hour later, Shannon was stretched out on her bed when she got a text from Haley. *Wanna talk?* Shannon tapped back. *Meet you on the*

Square. A bit later the girls dropped into the lawn. Shannon ripped out a fistful of grass and tossed it into the breeze. "I can't do anything right, Hale. Can't score, yelled at Abby, even got a red card."

"It's not your fault, Shan," Haley replied. "Remember, I can see the whole field. You run twice as much as any other player."

"Maybe I should join the cross country team."

Haley snorted. "The other girls need to do more, Shan."

"You saw what happened, Hale. I kept setting up girls in the box, and they sprayed the ball all over."

"Your red card means you can't play next week, Shan. Maybe the girls will step up."

"Let's hope so, Hale, or else this is gonna be a long season."

Later that night, Shannon checked the league website. The Swarm had one win, two losses, and one tie. They had dropped into sixth place out of eight teams. Shannon had slid to ninth in the scoring race. She thought of Chelsea, and checked the academy league website. The Wave was in first place, with four wins in four games. Chelsea led the league with ten goals.

Shannon got up and flopped on her bed. *Chelsea's doing great, so great she's forgotten about me.*

CHAPTER 6
'POOF'

AT THREE O'CLOCK IN THE morning, Shannon snapped out of her dream. She had been caught in a downpour, but it wasn't raindrops falling. It was red cards. Shannon sat up. *I got a red card. That's insane, just insane. I can't play in our next game. So what can I do? Work harder.*

Shannon drifted back off. When she woke again, a splash of sunlight lit her comforter. She sat up and tapped her ankle, sore, but only a little. In no time she threw on her soccer gear and scooted downstairs. Shannon toasted a piece of wheat bread, spread peanut butter on it, and poured a glass of grapefruit juice.

After she ate, Shannon filled her water bottle, grabbed her ball bag, and headed to the Square. Dots of dew clung to the grass, but she didn't care. She sat and did her stretches. Feeling loose, Shannon set ten orange cones in a crooked line across the Square. She set her watch. *Gotta beat twenty seconds*. Using only her right foot, she tapped through the cones. When she finished, her watch read 21:37. On her third try, she hit 19:28. Using only her left foot, it took Shannon five tries to beat twenty seconds. With both feet, on her first try she hit 18:36. On her second try, she beat that time by a full second.

After a few gulps of water, Shannon trotted behind the shed and grabbed the large thin board leaning against it. It was the size of the big goal, twenty-four feet wide by eight feet high. But it was not a perfect rectangle. Mr. Swift had cut squares out of each corner – four feet by four feet. Shannon dragged the board through the grass and leaned it in front of the big goal. Four targets, one in each corner.

Shannon set up ten balls along the chalk line eighteen yards from goal. One after another, she lashed them toward the opening in the upper left corner. Four shots smacked the board, three sailed over the bar, and three flew into the hole. *Not bad, but I can do better*. She put four in the upper right corner, five in the lower left, and six in the lower right. Shannon did the math. *Eighteen out of forty. Twenty, that's my target every time I do this.*

Her ball work done, Shannon set her mind on speed. *I'll do thirty-yard sprints across the Square, won't stop until I break five seconds.* She tore from chalk to chalk, but after nine sprints she had yet to hit her goal. She crouched, hit the button on her watch, and bolted off. Crossing the line, she saw 4.98 on her watch. Shannon pumped a fist. *Knew I could do it!*

Shannon walked inside and grabbed a water bottle from the fridge. As she took her first drink, the bottle fell from her hand and hit the floor. *That's weird, never done that before.* Shannon used paper towels to gather up the spilled water. Then she walked to the couch, flopped on, and dozed off for an hour.

On days the Swarm didn't practice, Shannon repeated this drill – dribble through cones, shoot, sprint. On Friday, she was legging out her last sprint when Tim walked up. "You're pushing yourself too hard, Shan."

"I got three girls on me," she shot back. "I have to lose 'em all."

"Your teammates are playing ten against seven," Tim countered. "They should be able to score, right?"

"But they don't score. That's why I have to do more."

"I get it, but don't run yourself into the ground," Tim warned.

Shannon followed Tim inside. Mrs. Swift was sticking a pizza in the oven. "I picked up a cool movie at the library," she said. "We'll watch it over pizza, thirty minutes."

Shannon went up, showered, and threw on shorts and a T-shirt. Joining her family in the kitchen, she found pizza and salads on the table. "Load up your plates, I'll put the movie on," Mrs. Swift said. Shannon took two slices and a bowl of salad and set up on the coffee table in the family room. The Swifts watched 'Victory,' a movie about Pele, the greatest soccer player ever. As a boy growing up in Brazil, Pele could not afford boots or a ball. He played barefoot in the streets with a ball made of rags stuffed into a sock. Shannon marveled at Pele's touch. He could dribble in any direction, with either foot, the ball never more than a step away.

Shannon was amazed to learn that Pele was the most famous athlete in the world. He was so popular that he even stopped a war. In 1967, Pele and his team traveled from Brazil to Nigeria to play two exhibition matches. There was one problem: Nigeria's government was fighting a war with the rebels of Biafra. But both armies were so excited to see Pele play that they agreed to stop fighting. After the games, Pele and his team returned to Brazil, and the war started again.

When the movie ended, Shannon stood. "Watching that fires me up to play. Sitting on the bench tomorrow, that's gonna hurt so bad."

"You're the captain, maybe you can help Coach Wiffle," Tim suggested.

Shannon nodded. "Coach asked me to take notes. She wants me to jot down what we do well and what we could do better."

"Good assignment," Mr. Swift said. "It will keep you occupied, so you don't fret about being on the bench."

Mrs. Swift went to the kitchen, came back,

and tossed a pad to Shannon. "Use that for notes, Shan."

Shannon eyed the pad. "I remember when you bought this at Staples, Mom. Hah, I never thought I'd be using it."

Shannon woke on Saturday, her eye on the tennis ball on her carpet. She slid out and whacked it into the wall. *I'll be so embarrassed today, sitting on the bench. I gotta disguise myself.*

Two hours later, Shannon left the house wearing sunglasses and a ball cap, her hair bunched up under the cap. At Freedom Park she sat at the end of the bench, notepad in one hand, pen in the other. The Swarm faced the Heat, the only unbeaten team in the league. The Swarm got an early break when a Heat back got whistled for a hand ball in the box. Coach called on Abby to take the penalty kick. Abby stepped up and pounded the ball – straight into the keeper's chest. Shannon stared into the grass. *I woulda scored. My red card has already cost us a goal.*

As the half wore on, the Heat took control. They scored off a corner kick and added a second goal on a knuckling smash from thirty yards. At halftime, the Swarm trotted off down by two. The girls gathered around Coach Wiffle. "I asked Shannon to take notes," Coach said. "Shan, what did you see?'

"Three times we passed up open shots from the edge of the box," Shannon said. "We're trying to dribble into the goal."

"Trust your shot, girls," Coach added. "In practice, you score often from twenty yards. I'll never yell at you if you take a promising shot, even if you don't score."

"What do you mean by, 'promising?'" Olga asked.

Coach thought about that. "A shot where you wouldn't be surprised to see the ball go in."

"Okay, now I get it," Olga said.

Coach swung her gaze back to Shannon. "You see anything else?"

Shannon eyed her notes. "We're watching our passes. We need to run off the ball."

Coach nodded. "Never admire your own pass, girls. Get free, be a target for your teammates."

Coach looked at Shannon. "That it?"

"We're losing the fifty-fifty balls," Shannon

went on. "We're watching the other team get there first."

By now, Olga was about to explode. "So, Shannon, what you're saying is, 'we stink.' Real helpful."

Shannon put up a hand. "We're doing lots of good things, too."

"That's right," Coach shot in. "Olga, you're beating your player to every pass. And Haley, you're coming off your line well, getting to crosses first."

Coach put out her hand and the girls stacked theirs on top. "Keep pushing, girls, the goals will come."

But they didn't. The Swarm lost, 3-0. Now they had one win, one tie, and three losses. They sat in seventh place, one rung from the bottom. As Shannon watched her teammates walk off, she felt a knot in her belly. *That loss was on me. No more red cards!*

On the ride home, Shannon got out her pen and pad and mapped out her training schedule for the week ahead.

Sunday   run three miles

Monday	one hour on the Square – sprints, dribbling, shooting
Tuesday	practice
Wednesday	run three miles, maybe four
Thursday	practice
Friday	run three miles

At the bottom, she scribbled these words: *I have to do more*

Shannon stuck to her plan on Monday and Tuesday. As she rode the bus home on Wednesday, she checked her school assignments. A three-page English paper was due the next day. She had written only the first paragraph. *Weird, how did I forget about that paper?*

A bit later Shannon sat at her desk, got out her notes, and began to write. Before long, she sensed her room growing darker. She looked out and saw a bank of black clouds gathering in the distance. Checking the weather app on her phone, she saw that heavy rain was on the way. *I better run before the storm hits.*

Shannon closed her notebook, changed into her running gear, and stretched on her carpet.

By the time she stepped outside, a cool breeze had kicked up. *Four miles, I can do this*. With the wind at her back, Shannon sailed through the first half. Starting on the return leg, she looked up at a dark sky. Now the wind blew in her face, but Shannon sliced through it. A hundred yards from her house, she broke into a sprint. Passing her mailbox, she checked her watch. Thirty-two minutes, a mile every eight minutes. She pumped her fists.

Shannon's timing was perfect. On her way up the driveway, large drops began to splatter on the pavement. By the time she reached the garage, it felt like nickels were falling. Shannon hustled in, guzzled some water, and wolfed down a bag of corn chips.

An hour later the Swifts sat down to pasta with red sauce and sausage. Shannon struggled to keep her eyes open. "Shan, you're as quiet as your fork," Mrs. Swift said as she passed a bowl of carrots to Tim.

"I got an English paper due tomorrow."

"Why did you put it off until tonight?" Mr. Swift asked.

"It snuck up on me."

Shannon pushed the pasta around her plate.

"You're not eating much, Shan," her mom said.

"I'm watching my weight," Shannon replied.

Mr. Swift made a sour face. "You have to eat to keep your strength up."

"Don't worry, Dad, I'm plenty strong."

"Who do you play on Saturday?" Tim asked.

"The Storm, it's a huge game. We haven't won since our first game. We can't go to England on a long losing streak."

"Speaking of England, don't you play against Chelsea Mills over there?" Tim asked.

"Maybe."

"That could be ugly," Tim needled. "The Wave is undefeated. Chelsea has something like twenty goals."

"Good, they'll be overconfident," Shannon shot back.

For dessert, Shannon had one spoonful of mint chocolate chip ice cream. She went upstairs and dug back into her English paper. After jotting two sentences, she surrendered to her eyes. She put her head on her desk and drifted off.

Two hours later, Shannon's mom jiggled her arm. "You fell asleep at your desk, Shan."

Shannon rubbed her eyes. "I gotta write my paper."

Still in a fog, she trudged to the bathroom and brushed her teeth. When she stepped back to her room, her feet led her to bed. *Just a quick nap, then I'll finish my paper.*

But there was nothing quick about this nap. When Shannon woke, she saw sunlight on her comforter. *My paper!* She sprang up, sat at her desk, and wrote as fast as she could. Skipping breakfast, she managed to finish the second page, leaving her one page short.

As Shannon bolted out the door, she saw Haley waiting on the sidewalk. Shannon ran up. "I gotta sit alone on the bus, Hale. Fell asleep early last night, gotta finish a paper."

"I told ya, Shan, you're pushing yourself too hard."

"Whatever," Shannon answered.

For the whole bus ride, Shannon wrote like mad. Her hand cramping up, she finished the third page as the bus rolled up at school. An hour later, her chest pounded as she handed in her paper. *I'm turning in a first draft, not good.*

On Friday morning, Shannon got her paper back. Scrawled at the top was a C minus, next to the words, *See me after class.* After the bell rang, Shannon approached Mrs. Smithers. "I'm worried about you," her teacher said. "Your paper was sloppy, misspelled words, clunky sentences. That's not like you, Shannon. Is something wrong?"

Shannon gazed at the floor. "I haven't been feeling well, Missus Smithers."

"I expect better from you, got it?"

"It won't happen again, Missus Smithers, promise."

Shannon stood and hurried out. *This is crazy. I have to do my work sooner. Can't let school get in the way of soccer.*

Shannon woke on Saturday, fired up to play her first game in two weeks. *Eighty minutes of pure energy, that's what I'll show the Storm.* But Shannon was in for a surprise. In the pre-game huddle, Coach Wiffle announced the starting lineup, and Shannon wasn't in it. "I'll put Shannon in after a few minutes," Coach said.

"My hope is the Storm won't be prepared to defend her right away."

When the game started, Shannon led the cheers. But inside, she burned. *Since when does the captain start the game on the bench?*

Coach's ploy appeared to backfire when the Storm scored in the third minute. Coach called Shannon over, and on the next throw-in she ran onto the pitch. The Storm coach took note. "Rachel, you're on eleven," she yelled out.

Shannon smiled inside. *Only one player marking me, hooray.* A minute later, Shannon ran down a loose ball in midfield. When Rachel challenged, Shannon slid the ball between her boots and built steam toward the box. The center back stepped up, and Shannon knifed past her.

The Storm's left back closed in, but Shannon was within range. She cocked her right leg and cracked a low rocket at the far corner. The keeper dove, but the ball whistled past her and punched the net. Her heart thumping, Shannon bolted up the flank, her teammates chasing her. "Great goal, Shan!" Abby yelped as she leaped on Shannon's shoulders.

But Shannon would have little time to savor her strike. The Storm coach called over two midfielders. "That number eleven, don't let her get the ball," she said. "If she gets it, shut her down, I don't care how."

When Shannon got the ball a minute later, she spun into a wall of Storm defenders. Seeing Montana streak down the right side, Shannon lofted the ball into her path. Shannon raced toward the box, three players in her midst. Montana crossed, but Shannon could not break through the crowd.

No matter where she went, Shannon felt trapped. She made lots of long runs off the ball, darting left then right, running away from the ball, and then back toward it. But each time she turned around, she found at least two defenders in her shadow.

In the stands, Tim marveled at Shannon's work rate. "Man, I'm breathin' hard just watching Shannon run."

Mrs. Swift nodded. "I don't know how she does it. It's kind of scary."

For all her effort, Shannon had little impact. Late in the half, she carved a path around four defenders and unleashed a rocket from twenty yards. But her shot actually helped the Storm. The ball slammed off the far post and bounced all the way outside the box. A Storm player collected and broke into open space.

Bent over and out of breath, Shannon watched the Storm forge a three-on-two counterattack. The player in the middle passed the ball wide left. The wing ran in and creamed a low laser under a diving Haley to tie the game.

At halftime Shannon was the last player to reach the bench. She grabbed her water bottle and drained it in one tilt. As Shannon sat, Coach neared. "Shan, your face is white. You need to sit for a while."

"No way, I'm fine," Shannon responded. Coach stared. "You sure?"

Shannon nodded. It was too much effort to speak.

In the second half, Shannon covered the field like morning dew. But halfway in, the Swarm caught another bad bounce. A Storm corner kick got knocked around in the box and struck Olga on the arm. The ref called a penalty kick. The Storm player shot low to Haley's left. She dove and tipped it, but it glanced off the post and into the goal. The Swarm trailed, 2-1.

As the clock ticked down, the Storm put the clamps on Shannon. Whenever she got the ball, two or three foes closed in. Shannon dished out precise feeds, but her teammates struggled to get the ball back to her. When the Swarm got a goal kick, Shannon looked toward her dad. He held up his index finger. *Only one minute left, I gotta do something.*

Shannon circled out near the corner flag. "Haley," she called, just loud enough for Haley to hear. Haley passed to Shannon. A girl charged at her. *Here I go.* Shannon dribbled around her first foe and then slashed between two more. When a fourth opponent neared, Shannon tapped the ball between her legs and shot by.

"Stop her!" yelled the Storm coach. As Shannon bolted up the flank, three more Storm players crowded her path. But Shannon would not be stopped. She slithered around those three and cut in toward the box. Looking up, she saw the keeper coming off her line. Shannon had already covered eighty yards. Could she finish this dazzling run with a goal? She dribbled into the box and cocked her leg, but the shot never came.

Shannon collapsed, her body plopping to the turf. The ref blew his whistle and ran over. Shannon did not move.

CHAPTER 7
DOCTOR'S ORDERS

TWO HOURS LATER, SHANNON'S EYES flicked open. She was in bed, but not her bed. She stared at the ceiling, an unfamiliar gray. A hand touched her arm, and she turned to see her mom. "Mom, where am I?" Shannon asked.

"We're at Manchester Hospital, Shan."

Shannon's eyes grew wide. "Why?"

"You collapsed on the field," her mom said. "You made this electrifying run, from box to box. You dribbled past seven players, I counted. But just as you were about to shoot, you tipped over like a sack of potatoes. And you didn't get up."

"Wow, I don't remember any of that. So what's wrong with me?"

"You're suffering from a case of exhaustion," her mom replied.

Shannon squinted. "What does that mean?"

"You pushed yourself too hard, and your body shut down."

"So, who won the game?" Shannon asked.

"The Storm, two to one," her mom said. "The ref ended it after you went down. It was almost over, anyway."

Shannon nodded at the tube attached to her arm. "What's that for?"

"It's called an IV," Mrs. Swift said. "It stands for 'intravenous,' which means, 'through your veins.' They're pumping you with fluids, mostly water, some nutrients. It'll help you recover."

A woman in a white smock stepped in. Shannon noticed her name tag, 'Doctor Willow.'

"Doctor, I thought I was in good shape," Shannon said. "So, why did I collapse?"

Doctor Willow sat on the bed. "Your mom says you've been training really hard, almost every day. I'm afraid you pushed yourself over the edge."

"My team's been losing," Shannon said. "I was just trying to do more."

Dr. Willow patted her arm. "I like your

spirit, Shannon. But you can't tax your body every day. Even professional athletes don't do that. Think about pro soccer players. They play a match on Saturday. They take Sunday off, and have a light practice on Monday. Pros give their bodies a break. You have to do that, too."

Shannon looked around the room. "Is there a scale in here?"

Dr. Willow tilted her head sideways. "Why do you need a scale?"

"I've been trying to lose a few pounds."

Dr. Willow put a hand on Shannon's arm. "You don't need to lose weight. From what your mom tells me, you do need to eat better."

"But I eat fine," Shannon protested.

"Your mom tells me you're skipping meals and eating unhealthy snacks between meals," the doctor replied. "Shannon, there's an old saying: 'You are what you eat.' When you eat right, you give your body fuel. When you eat wrong, you rob yourself of fuel. We're gonna make sure you're always fueled up."

Dr. Willow pulled a few pamphlets from her pocket. "Here's some info on healthy eating and exercise. When you follow these tips, you'll be in top shape, got it?"

"Got it. So when can I go home?"

The doctor checked Shannon's pulse. "I'm sending you home tonight."

Shannon smiled, but then Doctor Willow turned that smile into a frown. "I want you to rest for a full week. No running, and don't touch a soccer ball. You might miss a game or two, but you'll get your strength back."

Shannon looked at her mom. "Miss another game?"

Mrs. Swift nodded. "Doctor Willow knows best, Shan. Your body needs time to recover."

Shannon bit her lip, hard. *I'm already recovering, just ask my lip.*

A bit later, Shannon was on her last spoonful of chicken noodle soup when her dad and Tim walked in. "How are you feeling, Shan?" Mr. Swift asked.

"Much better, Dad, can't wait to go home." Shannon noticed streaks of dirt on Tim's white shorts. "How'd your game go?" she asked.

"We won, three-nil."

"At least one of us had a good day," Shannon cracked.

A few hours later, Shannon got released. This was her first visit to a hospital, and, she hoped, her last. *This place is eerie. Gray walls. Sad faces. The scent of medicine hanging in the air. At least they took care of me.*

Back at the house, Shannon found an envelope tucked in the front door, her name on it. She pulled out a note. *Shan, hope you're feeling better. That was an amazing run you made. I saw the whole thing – you left a trail of players all over the field! If you scored, I was thinking I might get an assist! Your BFF, Haley*

Shannon smiled. She followed her parents into the family room, where they sat on the couch. Mr. Swift put his arm around her. "Shan, it was really scary seeing you go down."

"I still can't believe it," Shannon said. "If I had lasted a few seconds longer, I coulda scored."

"Maybe so, but we never want that to happen again," Mr. Swift said. "That's why you're going to make some changes. From now on, after every practice and game, you will take a full day off."

"But Dad, I gotta be in top shape."

"You already are. You outrun every other player."

Shannon heard her stomach growl. "Mom, can you get me some chips?"

"I threw out all the junk, Shan. I'll get you an apple."

"Come on, Mom, one bag won't hurt."

"Chips are not a good source of energy, Shan."

"Okay, so what is?"

"You get most of your energy from carbohydrates," her mom said.

Shannon scrunched her face. "Carbo what?"

"Carbohydrates," Mrs. Swift repeated. "Bread, potatoes, pasta, and cereal are all good sources."

"I like all those foods," Shannon said.

Her mom nodded. "That's good, because you're going to eat lots of those things. From now on, you will eat a meal two hours before your games. That will give you energy, and it will give you time to digest what you've eaten."

"Coach gives you slices of oranges at halftime, right?" Mr. Swift asked

"Yeah, but I don't eat them," Shannon said. "I'm afraid they'll slow me down."

"You will eat them from now on," her dad said. "Good energy source."

"What about after games?" Shannon asked.

"That's when you need protein," Mr. Swift said.

"I like that word," Shannon said. "Sounds like 'pro team.'"

"Proteins will help your muscles recover," her dad went on. "Nuts and yogurt are good, so is Mom's trail mix."

"Cool."

Shannon stood. "Hang on," Mr. Swift said, "I'm not done. I want you to drink twenty-four ounces of water with your pre-game meal. At halftime, you drink another ten ounces of an energy drink. After the game, another twenty ounces of an energy drink."

Shannon sagged back into the couch. "Dad, I'll float away."

"Your body is seventy percent water," Mr. Swift said. "The way you run, you sweat off a lot of water. You have to hydrate – keep your water levels up."

Shannon rolled her eyes. "Carbohydrate, protein, hydrate, this sounds like science class. Can I be excused?"

"One more thing," Mrs. Swift added. "You know how you've said you want to cook more?

We'll find some healthy meals we can make together."

Shannon stuck up a thumb. "Haley's learning how to cook, she can help us."

Shannon got up and went into the kitchen. Her eye caught the newspaper on the table, opened to the sports page. The headline was huge.

MILLS LEADS WAVE TO ELEVENTH STRAIGHT VICTORY

Shannon sighed. *Maybe I'll quit soccer and become a chef.*

That night, Shannon was checking the league standings when her phone dinged, a text. *Shannon, I heard about your injury. I wish you a speedy recovery. I hope we get to see each other in England, maybe even meet on the field! Coach Dash.*

Shannon read the message twice, a smile crossing her face. *Wow, Coach Dash is awesome. Hope I get to see him in England.*

CHAPTER 8

SHANNON THE CHEF

FOR THE NEXT FIVE DAYS, Shannon moved in slow motion. She didn't run. She didn't touch a soccer ball. She climbed the stairs one at a time. Each day, she could feel her energy coming back. On her way home from the bus stop on Friday, Shannon felt the warm sun on her shoulders. She spotted her mom kneeling in the flower bed, pulling weeds. Shannon crept up behind her. "Boo!" she blurted.

Mrs. Swift flinched. "You scared the daylights out of me, Shan."

"I'm feeling much better, Mom. It's so nice out, can I go for a short run, pretty please?"

Mrs. Swift ran a sleeve over her forehead. "We're sticking with Doctor Willow's orders."

Shannon made a sour face. "I feel like a caged tiger."

"That cage will open soon, Shan. Hey, we're making dinner tonight, remember? Why don't you ask Haley to help pick out a meal? I'll take you both to the store so you can pick up the ingredients."

Shannon darted up to her room, shrugged off her backpack, and texted Haley. A few minutes later they met on the Square. "So Hale, what should we make for dinner?"

Haley tapped a finger on her chin. "We both love grilled cheese sandwiches, why don't we learn how to make one?"

"Good idea, but we can't make just a regular old grilled cheese. We gotta be creative, right?"

Haley took out her phone and did a quick search. Another smile edged across her face. "I got it!" Shannon waited a few seconds. "Okay, so tell me."

Haley smiled. "You'll see at the supermarket."

A bit later the girls piled into the car. On the way to the store, Haley tapped a list of items into her phone. Shannon tried to peek, but Haley shrunk back.

"Hale!"

"Come on, Shan, I know you like surprises."

When they reached the store, Mrs. Swift stayed in the car to make a call. She gave Shannon a twenty-dollar bill and the girls trotted in. Shannon grabbed a cart, and Haley jogged ahead to the bread aisle. By the time Shannon caught up, Haley had grabbed a loaf of whole wheat bread. She tossed it in the cart and tore around the corner to the dairy aisle, Shannon right behind. Haley flipped in a packet of sliced cheddar cheese. Checking her list, Haley darted over to the fresh fruit section. She inspected a bunch of apples, stuck two in a bag, and set it in the cart.

Haley checked her list. "One more item, Shan. Know where they keep the walnuts?"

Shannon thought for a second. "Walnuts, they must be hanging on a wall, right?"

Haley snorted. She asked a clerk, who told them to check the next aisle. Haley scooted over and grabbed a bag of shelled walnuts.

Twenty minutes later, the girls went to work in the Swifts' kitchen. Shannon got out four pieces of bread and spread mustard on one side of each slice. Haley cut the apples into thin slices. Shannon measured out one tablespoon of walnuts. The girls put the cheese, apple slices, and walnuts on a slice of bread, and laid a second slice on top.

Mrs. Swift dropped one tablespoon of butter into a small skillet and set it over a low flame. Shannon could hear the butter sizzle as her mom put the sandwich on the skillet. After a bit, Mrs. Swift used a spatula to turn up a corner of the sandwich. She smiled. "It's golden brown, time to turn it."

Mrs. Swift slid the spatula under the sandwich and flipped it over. She waited a minute, checked a corner, and flipped it again. "Both sides are golden brown," Shannon said. "How did you do that?"

"I've done it a thousand times, Shan. Your dad is the king of the grilled cheese."

Mrs. Swift set the cooked sandwich on a plate and gave the spatula to Shannon. "Okay, girls, your turn."

Shannon stuck a dab of butter on the skillet and watched it start to melt. Like her mom, she tilted the skillet left and right to spread the butter across the pan. Haley put the sandwich together and set it on the skillet. Shannon counted to twenty, and used the spatula to turn up a corner. "Not quite done," Haley said. Shannon let it cook a bit longer, and then she flipped it.

"Hey, pretty good!" Mrs. Swift said. Shannon handed the spatula to Haley. "I'll count to thirty," Haley said. She did, and then she flipped the sandwich over. The bread was golden brown. "We did it!" Haley exclaimed.

"Mom, that was a blast!" Shannon blared.

Mrs. Swift put the first two sandwiches in the oven to keep warm. "Okay, girls, three more to go." Shannon and Haley helped make three more sandwiches. Fifteen minutes later Shannon called out, "Dinner!"

Mr. Swift and Tim joined Shannon, Haley, and Mrs. Swift at the table. Tim was first to try the grilled cheese with apple and walnut sandwich. "Wow, Mom, this is really good," he said. Mrs. Swift pointed at the girls. "Thank Shannon and Haley, they made it."

Tim looked up. "No way."

"Yes, way," Shannon said. "Mom's teaching Haley and me how to cook."

Tim smiled. "That's awesome, now I got more people to make meals for me."

Shannon chuckled at that. But as the meal wore on, a question burned inside her. Finally, she found the courage to ask it. "Mom, I'm feelin' really good. Can I play half the game tomorrow?"

"No," Mr. Swift shot in. "Doctor's orders."

Haley looked at Mr. Swift. "Shan looks ready to me," she said. Mr. Swift set his eyes on Haley. "I appreciate your opinion, Doctor Punt," he said. "But Shannon is out until next week."

Shannon wanted to fight for it, but she knew she would lose.

At Freedom Park the next morning, Shannon sat on the bench for the second time in three matches. *I should've stayed home. When you can't play, it's torture to watch.* As it turned out, the game *was* torture to watch. Without Shannon, the Swarm struggled to build an attack. They gave up two late goals and lost, 2-0.

In the huddle afterward, Coach Wiffle tried to stay upbeat. "My word for the day is

'SPIRIT,'" she said. "You stayed positive until the final whistle. You talked to each other, you encouraged each other."

But Olga had grown tired of Coach's words. "You say that after every game, Coach. We can't score, and we keep losing."

"We did a lot of things well, Olga," Shannon cut in. "And here's the thing, girls. Next Saturday, we play the Wizards. They have the same record we do. We're gonna win, I guarantee it."

Olga smirked. "Shannon, did you have your brain checked at the hospital?"

"Come on, Olga," Shannon volleyed. "We gotta believe we can do it."

"Yeah, whatever," Olga muttered.

The following week, Shannon started her new routine. She went to two practices, ran three miles once, and took two days off. When Saturday morning rolled around, she felt fresh. As the Swifts reached the field, Tim turned to Shannon. "You gotta win today, make good on your promise."

Shannon sipped her water bottle. "Our team

is flat, Tim. I had to say something to pump us up."

"I get that, but don't try to do it all yourself," Tim said. "We've already seen that movie."

"Tim's right," Mr. Swift added. "Drink lots of water. Catch your breath after long runs." Finally, Mrs. Swift chimed in with, "Be sure to eat your orange slices at halftime."

By then, Shannon had rolled her eyes twice. *I'm getting triple-teamed again.* She bolted from the car in record time. Minutes later, she led the girls on a warm-up lap and through their exercises. Coach Wiffle called the team in and took a few seconds to look each girl in the eye. "Remember, if Shannon is surrounded, find the open player. Pass and move!" The players piled hands of top of Coach Wiffle's. "One, two, three, Swarm!"

Shannon had sat out two games, but the Wizards had not forgotten about her. Two minutes in, she gathered a ball in the circle and turned to find two defenders rushing at her. Abby ran into an open seam, and Shannon drilled the ball onto her foot. As Abby dribbled into the attacking third, Montana darted free down the right flank. Abby floated the ball toward the corner, and Montana collected and looked up. Shannon had raced to the edge of the box. "Now!" she yelled.

Montana chipped toward the far post. As Shannon ran in, the keeper charged out. Shannon leaped high and stuck her head at the ball. *Whomp!* Shannon and the keeper collided in mid-air. As Shannon thumped to the turf, she watched the ball bounce once and hit the net. Her heart going *boom-boom-boom*, she scrambled up and raced toward Montana, but then a whistled sounded. "No goal!" the ref yelled. "Foul on yellow, free kick, green."

Shannon ran up to the ref. "But I headed that in!" she protested.

"You ran into the keeper," the ref shot back.

"I headed the ball first!" Shannon argued.

The ref shook his head, and that really lit Shannon's fuse. "You blew that one, ref."

The ref tweeted his whistle and waved Shannon over. She hung her head. *Here we go again.* The ref pulled out his book and held a yellow card over Shannon. "But ref –"

"Shannon!" hollered Coach Wiffle. Shannon jogged away. *This is crazy. Even when I score, I don't score.*

A bit later, Shannon sprang Abby free in the box, but Abby cracked her shot off the bar. It was the best chance either team had in a scoreless half. At halftime, the girls huddled at the bench. Coach shook her fists. "Girls, I love the way you're passing and moving. Keep it up, we'll break through."

Shannon pulled out her water bottle and guzzled all ten ounces. She called Abby over. "Ab, you're faster than the girl marking you. I'll keep floating balls toward the corner." Abby nodded.

Early in the second half Olga headed a cross out of the box, and Shannon chased it down. She spun away from one girl and tapped the ball through the boots of another. Looking up, she saw something she hardly ever saw – an open field. Shannon exploded into top gear and gobbled up grass. As she neared the box, the girl marking Abby peeled off and ran at Shannon. Shannon rolled the ball ahead of Abby, sending her in alone.

The keeper ran out. Abby cut around her, but the ball rolled farther than she wanted. As the ball neared the end line, Abby tried to guide it between the posts. It rolled across the goalmouth, hit the far post, and settled a yard off the line. An alert Shannon had followed Abby's shot. She calmly tucked in the sitter, scoring the Swarm's first goal in almost forever. Shannon raced up the sideline, pumping her fists. The Swarm piled on her, celebrating like it was the first goal they had ever scored.

But the Wizards still had some magic left. They pushed more players up, trapping the Swarm in their own half. In the closing seconds, a corner kick ricocheted to a Wizard ten yards out. Olga slid for the ball, but met leg instead. The Wizard toppled over like a bowling pin. The ref blew his whistle and pointed at the penalty spot.

Olga thumped her fist on the ground. Shannon jogged over and helped her up. "You had to go for that ball, Olga."

"I blew it," Olga wailed. "Our chance to finally win, and I do that."

"Don't worry," Shannon said, "Haley will save us."

As a Wizard put the ball on the spot, Haley walked off her line and caught the girl's eye. In a voice just loud enough for the girl to hear, Haley said, "I'm stopping this."

Haley backed up to her line and slapped her gloves. As the shooter stepped toward the ball, Haley hopped to her left. The girl took the bait. She shot to Haley's right, but Haley was lunging back that way. She stuck out her hand as far as she could. Her chin hitting the dirt, Haley felt the ball tick her middle finger. It hit the post and bounced back in front, where Olga blasted it safely over the end line. Olga leaped on Haley. "Great save, Hale! You saved me!"

Seconds later, a Wizard launched a high corner kick that curled toward the back post. Haley stepped out, leaped over the crowd, and punched the ball out of the box. Montana gave it a good whack into the Wizards' end, and the ref blew the final whistle. The girls mobbed Haley, celebrating their first victory in six games.

On the sideline, the girls gathered around Coach Wiffle. She looked at Haley. "That penalty shot was headed right for the corner. How did you stop it?"

Haley held up her hand and pointed to the tip of her middle finger. "See how this finger is a little longer than the others? I touched that ball with only that finger, I swear."

Olga smiled. "I'm really glad you gave that

ball the finger." The girls hooted, while Coach Wiffle gave Olga the eye. Coach went on. "We had lost four straight games, but you keep on battling. My word for the day is, 'PERSEVERE.' I know, it's awkward and long. But it describes what you did – stick to your task when things were against you."

"Cool word, Coach," Abby said. "Too bad I'll never remember it."

The girls laughed, until Coach put up a hand. "So, next Saturday we play the Flash. And where do we go the weekend after that?"

"England!" the girls shouted.

Coach pulled a stack of papers from her backpack and asked Haley to pass it around. "This is our schedule for the next two weeks, let's run through it."

Shannon ran her eyes down the list.

Tuesday, May 7,	*quiz at practice, fun facts and figures, London and England*
Thursday, May 9,	*go over English money at practice*
Saturday, May 11,	*play the Flash*
Tuesday, May 14,	*crazy English words at practice (Coach's assignment)*

Friday, May 17, *players present on the bus to New York City*

Saturday and

Sunday, May 18-19, *Globetrotter Tournament, London*

Coach went through each item. "Do your homework on London," she said. "At practice on Tuesday, I expect you to crush my quiz."

CHAPTER 9
SHANNON UNLOADS

THE NEXT MORNING, A COOL wind stung Shannon's cheeks as she grabbed *The Manchester Mirror* off the front porch. She ducked inside and pulled out the sports section, her eye drawn to a huge color photo. In it, a tall girl with flowing red hair dribbled between two opponents. Shannon read the caption. *Chelsea Mills scored three goals to lead the Wave over the Gazelles, 4-1 yesterday. The Wave is now 14-0, and Mills leads the academy league with twenty-five goals and ten assists.* The photo and the story below it ate up half a page. Shannon sat and read the story. She found Chelsea's name eleven times.

Shannon searched for a story on her game. At last she found it, buried low in the corner on the back page. *Swarm wins, 1-0.* The story was four sentences short. Shannon flipped the paper on the table. *I could be playing for the Wave. But no, Chelsea is, and that scoundrel is the leading scorer on an undefeated team. Me? I'm playing for a team just one spot above the cellar.*

Mrs. Swift walked in. She nodded at the paper. "How's the story on your game, Shan?" she asked.

"It's more like a caption." Shannon held up the cover page. "But Chelsea Mills gets a huge photo and a huge story."

Mrs. Swift sat and read the caption under the photo. "Wow, Chelsea's really crushing it on the Wave."

Shannon drummed her fingers on the table. "I guess I blew it, Mom. I should've joined the Wave."

Mrs. Swift sat. "I know it's been a tough season, Shan. It's hard when you've got two or three players on you."

"I never thought I'd get this frustrated," Shannon said. "It's weird, sometimes I can't control my temper."

"Just keep trying your best, Shan. The tournament in England marks the end of the spring season. Who knows, that might be a good time to make a change."

Shannon tilted her head. "You mean, change teams?"

"You never know, Shan."

Mrs. Swift changed the subject. "So today is National Peanut Butter and Jelly Day. You ready to whip up a peanut butter and jelly smoothie?"

"You know it!"

Mrs. Swift scribbled out a list and stuck it under the magnet on the fridge door. Shannon eyed the list. She opened the freezer and took out a box of strawberries. Next, she took from the fridge a carton of low-fat strawberry yogurt. Her mom set the blender and a measuring cup on the counter. Shannon spooned the yogurt into the blender. Next, she filled the cup with berries and dumped them in.

Mrs. Swift handed Shannon a jug of milk and another measuring cup. "Pour out eight ounces." Shannon found a line marked, '8 oz.' *'Oz', that's weird.* "Mom, there's no 'zee' in the word 'ounces,' so why is it abbreviated with, 'oh-zee?'" she asked.

"Good question, Shan. That abbreviation was borrowed from an old Italian word, 'onza.'"

Shannon's mouth fell open. "Mom, you're like the wizard of 'oz', get it? How could you know that?"

"I wondered the same thing once, so I looked it up."

Shannon filled the cup to eight ounces and poured the milk over the strawberries and yogurt. Her mom handed her a tub of peanut butter and a tablespoon. Shannon scooped out two tablespoons of peanut butter and added it to the mix. Mrs. Swift peeked in the blender. "Good to go," she said as she put the lid on. Shannon turned it on and watched her breakfast spin to life. Seconds later she shut it off and poured the smoothie into a tall glass. She took her first sip, and smacked her lips. "Mom, so scrumptious!"

Mrs. Swift stuck up a thumb. "That's a quick and healthy breakfast, takes only four ingredients and five minutes. It has plenty of protein, calcium, and other nutrients – instant energy."

Shannon took another gulp. "Bet we can make all kinds of smoothies."

"We can get real creative, Shan. Next time,

we'll use crushed sunflower seeds instead of peanut butter."

"Sunflower, I love that word," Shannon said. "Two beautiful things, together in one word."

After she finished her smoothie, Shannon climbed the stairs and sat at her computer. She did a search on 'London,' and jotted notes on her pad. *Wow, Coach was right, London's a cool city. There's so much to see, all from the top of a double-decker bus!*

After practice on Tuesday, the girls gathered by the bench. Coach Wiffle pulled a slip of paper from her pocket. "Okay, time to see who's done their homework. Who can tell me when London was founded?"

"In the first century, by the Romans," Haley said.

"Very good!" Coach said. "That's almost two thousand years ago."

Abby raised a hand. "Hang on, Coach, that means London is almost ten times older than the United States. That can't be right."

"Yes it can, Abby. That's why people refer to England as, 'the motherland.'"

Coach checked her sheet. "Who can tell me how many languages are spoken in London?"

"Twenty?" Shannon guessed.

"Try three hundred," Coach replied.

"Wow," Shannon said, "I didn't know there were that many languages in the world."

Coach checked her sheet. "How many people live in London?"

"Eight million," Montana replied.

"Very good!" Coach raved. "By the way, who knows the city with the most people?"

Erin raised a hand. "Delhi, in India, twenty-five million people."

"Nope," Olga countered, "it's Jakarta, in Indonesia. They have thirty million."

"You're both wrong," Shannon cut in. "It's Tokyo, Japan, with thirty-seven million."

Shouts followed. "Tokyo!" "Jakarta!" "Delhi!" Coach put up a hand. "Okay, what did we just learn?"

"That no one agrees on the world's biggest city," Haley said.

"Yes, but we also learned something about the Internet," Coach said. "You can't trust it! You just came up with three different answers to the same question. How crazy is that?"

"It's crazy all right," Abby agreed. "So how do know when you have the right answer?"

"You check different sources," Coach replied. "See if you find one answer that is more common than others. And remember, whenever you use the Internet for any paper you write, be sure to note where you get your information."

Haley stuck up a hand. "So, Coach, you didn't tell us, which city has the most people?"

Coach smiled. "I did my homework, and I'd say, Tokyo, Japan."

At practice two days later, Coach ended the scrimmage early. As the girls gathered, Coach opened her backpack and took out a baggie with coins and paper in it. "Okay, who is planning to buy a few things in England?"

Hands shot up. Coach asked, "How are you going to pay for what you buy?"

"With my money," Olga replied.

"Not so fast, Olga. Some shops over there don't take dollars."

Coach took a slip of paper from her baggie and held it up. "Anyone know what this is?"

"It's a one-pound note," said Montana. "We

have dollar bills. In England, they have pound notes."

"Right," Coach said. She fished a few coins out of her baggie. "Like us, England has coins. But they don't call coins, 'cents.' They say, 'pence.' There are a hundred pence in a pound."

"So when we say fifty cents, they would say fifty pence?" Abby asked.

"You got it, but there's one more difference. The English abbreviate pence to 'pee.' So if you buy something that costs 50 pence, the clerk will say, 'Fifty pee.'"

Coach passed out a few coins, and the girls took turns inspecting them.

"How come every coin has this woman's face on it?" Shannon asked.

"That's the Queen of England," Coach Wiffle said.

"She must be important," Shannon followed.

"The queen is the face of England," Coach said. "When the time comes to honor the men and women of England who died fighting in wars, the queen would lead that event. If England wins a big international soccer match, she would lead the celebration."

Abby nodded. "The queen kind of shows the mood of the country."

"Pretty good, Abby, you come up with that yourself?" Coach asked.

"Sort of, I read it on the Internet."

The girls whooped.

"One more thing, girls," Coach said. "We leave for England in eight days. Has everyone finished their projects?"

Every girl raised a hand.

On Saturday morning, Shannon rode to the field with her parents and Tim.

"Shan, you could be in for a tough day," Tim said. "I read about the Flash in the paper. They've won every game. They've outscored their opponents by something like twenty-eight goals to four."

"Good," Shannon snapped. "They'll be cocky."

At the field thirty minutes later, Shannon was passing with Abby when the ref called for the captains. Shannon jogged toward the circle. The Flash captain was already there. "Shake hands, girls." Shannon put out her hand and her opponent shook it, real hard. Shannon tried to free her hand, but the girl tightened her grip. Finally, the girl let go.

The ref took a coin out of her pocket. "Don't bother to flip it," said the Flash captain. "Let them kick off. It may be the only time they have the ball."

Shannon felt her heart flap. To the ref she said, "Just flip the coin, I'll call it."

The ref flicked the coin, and Shannon called tails. It landed on tails. Shannon stared into the eyes of the Flash captain. "We'll take the ball," she said.

Shannon jogged back to the huddle and told the girls about the coin flip. Abby smacked her hands together. "Okay, girls, time to flush the Flash!"

The Swarm kicked off. Shannon played the ball wide to Abby, but the left back tackled it away. The back smashed a long ball high up the flank. As the Flash wing chased it down, Shannon felt a sneaky shove in the back. Her mark took off toward the box. Shannon raced to catch up, but she lagged a few yards behind. "Olga, help!" she called out.

Olga edged toward Shannon's player, giving

her mark a lane into the box. The girl dribbled in and fired a low dart that stung the far post. It kicked back into the box, where Haley dove on it. Shannon took a deep breath. *Whoa, this team can play. And this team cheats.*

Shannon controlled Haley's punt and turned to find only one player on her. She tucked the ball through the girl's boots and burst into the circle. Seeing Montana break free out wide, Shannon played the ball ahead of her. Montana gathered and built speed, and Shannon broke toward the box. "Montana!" she yelled.

Montana pushed the ball into Shannon's path. Shannon ran onto it and cut free in the box. She had only the keeper to beat, but her angle was tight. Out of the corner of her eye, she spotted Abby racing in from the far side. Shannon cocked her leg, dropping the keeper to her knees. But then she slid the ball into Abby's path ten yards from goal. All Abby had to do was tap the ball home, but she swung too hard and blasted it over the bar.

Abby sank to her knees. Shannon ran up. "Keep your back straight, Ab, you'll get the next one."

Later in the half, Shannon swept up a loose

ball in the circle. She wriggled past two foes and charged toward the box. When the center back slid over to challenge, Shannon set up Montana for a clean look inside the eighteen. Montana shot, but the ball banged off the keeper's shins and skittered back outside the box. Shannon threw up her hands. *No one on this team can score!*

Just before halftime, Shannon caught a lucky break. A Flash defender slipped as she tried to clear the ball. It rolled straight to Shannon, twenty-five yards from goal. She tapped the ball once and unleashed. The keeper took one step and dove, but the ball rocketed over her arms and punched the roof of the net.

Shannon started to run, but Abby tackled her and her teammates piled on. Shannon's sizzling strike gave the Swarm a 1-0 lead that held until halftime. As Shannon jogged off, Coach Wiffle greeted her. "What a treat to be covered by only one player, huh?" Coach asked. "Yeah," Shannon replied. "Hope it keeps up."

But it didn't. The first time Shannon got the ball in the second half, she was seeing double. She played the ball back to Olga, who swung it wide to Abby. Abby zipped down the flank and sent a long ball toward Montana, whose volley from fifteen yards sailed inches wide.

"Wake up, Flash!" screamed their coach. And with those angry words, the game changed. The Flash began to win every loose ball. They strung passes together, keeping the Swarm in constant pursuit. As the half wore on, the Swarm wore out. The Flash scored twice, taking the lead with ten minutes to play.

Shannon had been fenced in the whole second half. She was running out of patience, but not her will to win. Shannon strayed from her mark and stole a pass. She tapped to Abby in the circle and broke free on the flank. Abby tried to feed back to Shannon, but an opponent cut the ball off. Shannon's frustration boiled over. She snapped, "Abby, you can't –," but then she ate the rest of the sentence.

Minutes later, Shannon stripped the ball from a defender. She dribbled toward the box, her eye picking up Abby cutting in from the flank. When the last defender met Shannon, she led Abby with a soft feed in the box. Abby ripped a shot, but it sailed wide. Shannon bit her lip, hard. *Passing is a waste of time, I gotta do it myself.*

Shannon looked toward her dad. He put up one finger. *One minute to even the score.*

The Flash keeper launched the goal kick high above the circle. Shannon settled under it, leaped, and headed wide to Montana. As Montana juked around a defender, Shannon burst down the right flank. Montana spooned the ball into Shannon's path, and she gathered it at the corner of the box.

Shannon had one defender between her and the goal. To her left she saw Abby racing in, unmarked. "Shannon!" Abby called. Shannon cocked her leg as if she was about to feed Abby. But on her down swing she curled the outside of her boot into the ball, pushing it into free space to her right. Shannon took one more step and unloaded. The defender lunged and got her boot on the shot. It trickled into the keeper's hands. The ref blew his final whistle. The Swarm lost, 2-1.

As the Flash players celebrated, Abby ran up to Shannon. "I was wide open!"

"I thought I could beat that girl."

"Yeah, and look what happened," Abby snapped. "You blew it."

Shannon's eyes flared. "I set you up all

game, Abby. You coulda scored five goals. I wasn't going to watch you miss another one."

Abby stormed off. Shannon stared at the grass. *Wish I could dig a hole and crawl into it.* At last, Shannon walked over and joined the huddle around Coach Wiffle. "I'm proud of your effort, girls," Coach said. "You gave that team all they could handle."

"We shoulda done better," Abby ranted. "But we forgot how to play like a team."

Olga piled on. "Yeah, Shannon tried to do it all herself."

Coach fired her clipboard into the grass. "Stop criticizing each other!" She paced, searching for words. Shannon wanted to say something, but the lump in her throat kept rising. Finally, Coach found her voice. "Look, we just gave the best team in the league all it could handle. We're just in a rut around the goal. Keep hustling, and the goals will come. See you Tuesday."

Shannon picked up her bag and walked to her family. Her dad hugged her. "You played a whale of a game, Shan." Shannon kicked a rock across the lot. "It doesn't matter what I do. If I pass, we don't score. If I try to do it myself, I'm a ball hog."

They got in the car, and Tim turned to Shannon. "You coulda had six assists today, but your teammates couldn't hit the ocean from the beach. Face it, Shan, you're too good for this team."

Shannon plucked a piece of dirt off her knee. "I lost it at the end. Abby scolded me for not passing. I sassed her for not scoring. Now she hates me."

"She doesn't hate you," her dad said. "She's frustrated too. I'm sure she feels bad about not scoring on some of your great passes."

Shannon blew out a long breath. "I hate it when people are mad at me."

Mrs. Swift faced Shannon. "You should apologize to Abby," she said. "That's what captains do."

Shannon closed her eyes for the rest of the ride home.

That night, Shannon paced in her room. *I gotta call Abby, but what do I say?* She sat at her desk and wrote some notes. She made the call, and Abby answered.

"Abby, it's Shannon. I'm sorry about the last play."

"It's okay," Abby said, her voice low.

"No, it's not. I shoulda passed. And I shouldn't have sassed you after the game."

"I was trying my best," Abby said.

"I know, and you probably would've scored."

"Shan, forget about it," Abby said. "Besides, I wasn't so nice either. Sorry about what I said."

"You were right to be mad, Ab," Shannon replied. "I'll never do it again, okay?"

"It's all good, Shan. Thanks for calling."

Shannon hung up, feeling like she had swept away one dark cloud. Her phone dinged, an email from Coach Wiffle. *Girls, you played your best game of the season today. As for what happened at the end, forget about it. Soccer is a tough game, where you have to make decisions in a hurry. Let's not judge. No one was right or wrong. My word for the day is, 'MOMENTUM.' It means we are going to England with increasing speed and strength. Go Swarm!*

Shannon hit the reply button. *Coach, I'm sorry*

for what I did at the end of the game. I probably should have passed to Abby, and I shouldn't have yelled at her. I called her and said I was sorry. When we go to England next weekend, I'll be a team player, and be the captain I should be. I hope we get a chance to play the Wave. If we do, I will play my best game ever.

Shannon sent the message and flopped on her bed. *I'm trying to stay positive, but this has been the worst season of my life. Am I stuck on the Swarm forever?*

CHAPTER 10

BANGERS, BOBBIES, AND BRACES

O N TUESDAY, COACH WIFFLE ENDED the scrimmage early and called the girls in. She pulled a sheet of paper from her jacket pocket. "Okay, it's time to have fun with words. A few weeks ago, I said we were, 'knackered.' Who remembers what it means?"

"It means, 'tired,'" Abby said. "I'll use it in a sentence. Learning new words really knackers me out."

The girls hooted. Even Coach failed to pinch back a smile. She went on. "Many of the words we use have different meanings in England. Let's start with your favorite sport."

"Soccer?" Shannon guessed.

"It's called soccer here, but in England they call it 'football,'" Coach said. "Makes sense, right? The feet are used much more in soccer than in American football." Shannon nodded. *Wow, I hadn't thought about that.*

Coach eyed her list. "Here's another one. In England, a truck is called a 'lorry.'"

"Hey, that's my sister's name," Montana said. "I didn't know she was a truck."

The girls howled. Coach checked her list and pointed at Erin. "See how Erin's hair falls over her forehead? We call that bangs, but in England they call it, 'fringe.'"

Coach checked her list. "Here's another one, braces."

Abby pointed at Montana. "Montana just got braces. She likes Mark Gibson, but he has braces, too. She's afraid that if they kiss, their braces might lock up. Who wants to walk around school with a boy attached to your face?"

Montana chased Abby but couldn't catch her. Coach Wiffle raised a hand. "In England, braces hold up your pants. We call them suspenders."

Coach rolled on. "If you order fish and chips in England, what do you get?"

"Fish and potato chips?" Shannon guessed.

"Good try, but in England, chips are French fries," Coach explained.

"So, what do they call potato chips?" Shannon asked.

"Crisps."

"Crisps?" Abby repeated. "I can barely say that word. It rhymes with 'lisp.'"

Coach rolled her eyes. "Okay, what are police officers called in England?"

"Cops?" tried Haley.

"Good guess, but they're called 'bobbies.' The English police were founded by a man named Robert Peel. 'Bobby' is short for Robert."

Coach folded the sheet and put it in her pocket. "Wait," Haley said, "I've got one. How do English people say the last letter in the alphabet?"

"Zee," Olga tried.

"Nope, they say, 'zed.' Rhymes with red," Haley said.

"Very good, Haley!" Coach blared.

Coach reached into her backpack, pulled out another stack of papers, and passed it along. "That's our schedule for the trip, be sure you give a copy to your parents."

At home that night, Shannon dropped onto the couch and studied the schedule.

Friday	Arrive at night
Saturday	Eleven a.m., first game versus Holland
	One p.m., lunch, Bull & Bear Pub
	Tour Buckingham Palace, Changing of the Guards
	Four p.m., second game versus Spain
Sunday	Ten a.m., third game versus Ireland
	Tour Trafalgar Square/Big Ben
Monday	9 a.m., championship game
	Return home

Shannon noticed the *Manchester Mirror* on the coffee table. *Wonder if there's an article about the tournament.* She opened the sports page and saw the headline.

NEW JERSEY WAVE TO COMPETE IN GLOBETROTTER TOURNAMENT

Shannon read. The story rambled on about the Wave. Their perfect record, eighteen wins and no losses, and their "superstar," Chelsea Mills. Finally, Shannon came to the last paragraph. *One other local team is competing in the tournament, the Swarm. They have struggled this year, winning only two of their eight games.* Shannon folded up the paper. She stood and tossed it into the air. When it floated down, she blasted her right foot into it, sending sheets flying off in different directions.

Mr. Swift had walked in just as Shannon punted. "That's the first time I've seen a newspaper used as a soccer ball," he said. "Another story about Chelsea Mills?"

"Yup. I want to play the Wave so bad in England."

"American teams do well in international tournaments, Shan," her dad said. "I have a feeling you'll get that chance."

That night, Shannon stood in front of her mirror and practiced her presentation on Trafalgar Square three times. After the last one, she figured she was ready to go.

Three days later, Swarm players and their families gathered for goodbyes in the school parking lot. As Shannon hugged her parents she tried to ward off tears, but a few dribbled out.

She and her teammates boarded a bus, along with Coach Wiffle and a chaperone, the social studies teacher, Mr. Bloomer.

Once the bus reached the highway, Coach grabbed a microphone. "It's time for your presentations, girls. Let's start with the three places we will visit – Trafalgar Square, Big Ben, and Buckingham Palace, for the Changing of the Guard. Shannon, you have Trafalgar Square. You go first."

Coach handed Shannon the microphone. "Trafalgar Square sits in the middle of London," she began. "It has lots of statues, but my story isn't about statues, it's about birds."

Abby had closed her eyes, but when she heard "birds," she perked up. Shannon went on. "My mom and dad visited Trafalgar Square before I was born. Thousands of pigeons were flying around. Tourists were buying bird seed from vendors. The tourists would scatter the seeds on their arms and hats. The pigeons would swoop down and peck away. My mom had so many birds on her, my dad walked past her and didn't recognize her."

"Did it hurt, getting pecked like that?" Abby asked.

"My mom says she was laughing so hard, she didn't feel any pain."

"How cool!" Montana blared. "Can we do that?"

"Nope," Shannon said. "The birds aren't there anymore."

"What?" Abby cried. "Why not?"

"The mayor of London said the pigeons were a menace," Shannon explained. "They carry lots of bad stuff – like influenza and Lyme disease. Plus, it cost a hundred thousand dollars a year to clean up all the droppings. So, the mayor said bird seed couldn't be sold anymore."

"But that's not fair to the birds," Abby whined. "If a bird's gotta poop, you can't blame the bird."

Shannon snorted. "The birds had a favorite target, a statue of some guy named Lord Nelson. He led the English Navy to a victory over Napoleon of France, like two hundred years ago. Lord Nelson's statue is almost two hundred feet tall, so that's a lot of poop to clean."

"Did people get angry when the mayor stopped the sale of seed?" Abby asked.

"You better believe it," Shannon said. "The

mayor was going to announce his plan right there in Trafalgar Square. But people said they would dump buckets of bird droppings on his head, so he had to cancel his announcement."

Shannon checked her notes. "One more thing about birds. During the first world war, England used pigeons to take messages to soldiers. Pigeons could fly very fast and very far – almost a mile a minute for hundreds of miles without rest. Over half-a-million pigeons were used to pass messages between troops and special agents. That's why Germany ordered all birds headed to Britain to be shot out of the sky."

Shannon passed the microphone to Coach. "Great job, Shan," Coach said. Coach checked her list. "Now we go from pigeons to pennies. Abby, tell us about Big Ben."

Abby took the microphone. "Big Ben is the nickname for the clock tower in the heart of London. It is London's best known landmark, kind of like the Empire State Building in New York."

Abby checked her notes. "Big Ben is the largest four-faced chiming clock in the world.

It stands three hundred and twenty feet tall, that's like a soccer field standing on end."

"Can we go up to the clock?" Olga asked.

"It's not open to the public," Abby said.

"That stinks," Olga whined.

"You wouldn't want to go up there anyway," Abby said. "There's no elevator. You'd have to climb three hundred and thirty-four stairs."

Montana put up a hand. "So, Abby, what about the pennies?"

"Chill, Montana, I'm getting there," Abby said. "The clock's faces are twenty-three feet wide, about the same width as a soccer goal. During the world wars, the faces were kept dark at night. That way, enemy pilots could not use the lights as a guide into the center of London."

Abby saw Montana holding up a penny. "Okay, Montana, the pennies. For Big Ben, time is kept by a pendulum that swings back and forth. Workers keep a stack of pennies on top of the pendulum. If the clock is going a bit too slow, they add a penny to the stack. That speeds up the clock by two-fifths of a second each day. If the clock is running too fast, they take a penny off the stack."

Coach raised her hand. "Why is the tower called, 'Big Ben?'"

"Good question, student Wiffle," Abby said, and the girls snickered. "Some people think the tower was named after Sir Benjamin Hall, who installed the Great Bell in the tower. Others say it was named after Benjamin Caunt. He was a heavyweight champion boxer in England back then."

Coach led the cheers for Abby. Abby bowed and returned to her seat. As the bus chugged closer to New York, the girls ran through their presentations. As they neared New York City, only Haley had not presented. "I have an idea, Haley," Coach said. "Since you're presenting on food, let's do yours at lunch tomorrow in London."

Minutes later, the bus rolled onto the George Washington Bridge spanning the Hudson River. Half way across the bridge, the girls left New Jersey and entered New York. A blue sky gave them a clear view of the hundreds of buildings jutting high into the air. Shannon tapped Coach on the shoulder. "I'm sure London is cool, but I bet no city can match New York's buildings."

"New York has a fabulous skyline," Coach

agreed. "Lots of tall buildings, and they all look different. But when it comes to history, few cities can match London."

Olga made a face. "Coach, why are you so big on history? I mean, that's all in the past."

Coach smirked. "You can learn from the past, Olga."

"Coach, you sound like a teacher."

"I am a teacher!"

"But you're not a history teacher."

Coach rolled her eyes. "Olga, sometimes you make me crackers."

Olga tilted her head. "Crackers?"

"In England, it means, 'crazy.'"

A bit later, the bus rolled up at Kennedy Airport. The girls checked their bags and passed through the security gates. Later they boarded the plane, taking up the last three rows. Once the jet reached cruising altitude, Coach stood and faced the girls. "Big day tomorrow," Coach said. "We play a team from Holland in the morning. After that, we eat lunch in The Bull and the Bear."

Erin shot Coach a look. "The Bull and the Bear, is that a zoo?"

"No, it's a pub," Coach said.

"So, what's a pub?" Olga asked.

"Pub is short for public house," Coach said. "It's a place where people go to eat and drink. They're like restaurants, and they have cool names. The most popular pub names are The Red Lion, The Crown, The Royal Oak, and The Swan. My favorite pub names are The Fox and the Hound, and The Crooked Chimney."

"I can't wait to eat some bangers and mash," Haley said.

Montana made a face. "What the heck is that?"

"You'll find out tomorrow when Haley presents at the Bull and Bear," Coach said. "After lunch, we'll visit Buckingham Palace to see the Changing of the Guard."

Haley looked at Coach. "We're going to have a little fun at Buckingham Palace." Coach tipped her head sideways, and Haley went on. "You know how the guards are supposed to stand still and never change their expression? Well, Shannon and I are going to make a guard crack up."

Coach gave Haley a look. "Haley Punt, what are you up to?"

"Sorry, Coach, can't ruin the surprise."

CHAPTER 11

BIG LAUGHS AT BUCKINGHAM PALACE

WHEN SHANNON WOKE THE NEXT morning, she thought her eyes were playing a trick. *Why is my pillow white, not purple? Hey, where am I?* She rolled over and saw Haley sleeping in the other bed. *That's right, we're in London.* Shannon checked her watch. It was eight in the morning in London, but only three in the morning in New Jersey. *Wow, no wonder I feel tired. Now I know what jet lag is.*

A bit later, Shannon thought she heard Haley stir.

"Hale, you awake?"

Haley rolled over. "Yup, my alarm clock just asked, 'Hale, you awake?'"

Shannon snorted at that. "Sorry, Hale. So,

you said we're gonna make a guard crack up today. What are you getting me into?"

Haley swung out of bed. She walked over to her suitcase and pulled out an inflated rubber cushion. It was the size of a small frying pan. "My brother gave me this, it's called a Whoopee cushion," Haley said. "Watch this." She put the cushion on the floor and sat on it. The air escaped out of the hole, and Shannon giggled. "That sounds like a loud fart, Hale. But how are you gonna do it?"

"You mean, how are *we* gonna do it. Come on, let's go through the plan." The girls practiced the routine they would follow in front of the guard. After a few tries, they had it nailed.

A bit later, Coach Wiffle led the girls down to the café off the lobby. They filled a large table, and Coach ordered first. "I'll have the full English," she said.

Shannon shot Coach a puzzled look. "The full English, say what?"

"Eggs, bacon, sausage, mushrooms, and baked beans," Coach explained.

"Mushrooms and baked beans for breakfast?" Shannon replied. "Coach, are you crackers?"

Coach smiled. "Look, we have a busy day,

two games and a visit to Buckingham Palace. The full English will keep me full of energy."

"The baked beans scare me, Coach," Abby said. "Don't sit near me at lunch."

The girls howled. After breakfast, they dashed ahead of Coach into the lobby. "You're going the wrong way," Coach called out. "The lift is this way."

"The lift?" Haley said. "Oh, yeah, the elevator."

Ten minutes later, Shannon and Haley were in their uniforms, stretching on the carpet in their room. "I'm so fired up to play, Hale. Nobody knows me here, so I won't get double-teamed."

"I know this has been a rough season for you, Shan. You've worked so hard, but the girls haven't helped you much."

"We've had tons of bad luck, Hale. How many posts and crossbars have we hit? How many handballs did we give away in our box? By now, luck should be on our side."

Haley nodded. "It would be wild if we played the Wave in the final. You think we could beat 'em?"

Shannon slapped the carpet. "Of course we

can beat 'em!" Shannon held up her palm, and Haley gave her five.

It was ten-thirty when the Swarm got off the bus at the field. Shannon led the girls on a few laps around the chalk and then through their stretching routine. She was passing with Abby when the ref blew her whistle and called for captains. Shannon jogged out to meet the Holland captain. The girl wore all orange, the color of Holland's national team uniform. She even had a large orange circle painted on her cheek. Shannon felt anxious. *How good are these girls? Will they bottle me up?*

Shannon lost the flip and trotted back to the huddle. Coach swung her eyes from girl to girl. "Listen, we flew almost four thousand miles. This is our chance to end our spring season on a positive note. Now how about an Orange Crush?" Coach put out a hand, and the girls stacked theirs on top. "One, two, three, Swarm!"

Thirty seconds into the match, Shannon stole a pass in the circle. She burst out wide, cut around two players, and blazed into the corner. Nearing the line, Shannon swung into a powerful cross that sailed toward the far post. Abby darted inside her mark and smashed the ball inches under the bar for the first goal. Minutes later, Shannon stole a pass and weaved around two defenders near the edge of the box. Her eyes up, she thumped a laser into the far corner. Just before halftime, Shannon rose high and nodded in Abby's corner kick to put the Swarm up 3-0. At the break, Shannon jogged off with a smile. *Wow, it's nice to be way ahead for a change.* Coach Wiffle rested Shannon for the final twenty minutes, and the Swarm cruised to a 4-1 win.

Later that afternoon, the girls gathered around Coach Wiffle and Mr. Bloomer in the hotel lobby. "Girls, Haley is our expert on English food," Coach said. "She's ready to serve up some cool info, so let's eat!" Coach led the girls out the revolving door. They walked two blocks before Shannon saw the sign for the Bull and the Bear Pub across the street. As she stepped off the curb, Mr. Bloomer yelled, 'Shannon!" Shannon leaped back onto the curb as a car shot past. Shannon put a hand on her head. "I looked for cars, but I got confused."

"You looked the wrong way," Mr. Bloomer said. "Remember, cars drive on the left over here. You need to be extra careful."

Shannon nodded. *Wow, that was scary.* Inside the pub, the girls took seats around a large table. Olga looked at the menu. "Okay, Haley, bangers and mash, what's the deal?"

"The bangers are sausages," Haley began. "The mash is mashed potatoes. The dish is smothered with a mushroom and onion gravy."

"Why do they call sausages, 'bangers?'" Olga asked.

"Because you have to pierce them while they're cooking," Haley said. "If you don't, they will burst, or go 'bang.'"

Shannon eyed the menu. "What about bubbles and squeak?"

"That's a dish made from cold vegetables left over from another meal," Haley explained. "It starts with potato and cabbage. You can add carrots, peas, Brussels sprouts, and other vegetables. The vegetables are fried in a pan, together with the mashed potatoes. 'Bubbles and squeak' describes what you see and hear during the cooking process."

"English people sure like to mash their potatoes," Shannon commented.

Montana scanned the menu. "So, Hale, what's a 'Toad-in-the-hole?'"

"That's a sausage link covered in batter and roasted," Haley said. "The sausage is the 'toad.' It sits in the 'hole' between the batter below and the batter above. We call it, 'pig in a blanket.'"

The waiter came, and Coach ordered first. "I'll have the Ploughman's lunch."

The girls looked at her. "Big hunk of bread, big hunk of cheese," Coach said. "How easy is that?"

After the girls finished their main courses, each one had a chocolate biscuit for dessert. Coach paid the bill. "Okay, we're off to Buckingham Palace, can't wait to see what Haley is up to."

The girls stepped out to the street and waited until a double-decker bus pulled up. Coach led the way up a flight of stairs. The girls took the seats on the second floor, which had no top. "So cool," Shannon said, "you can see everything."

The bus roared into a busy area teeming with theatres, shops, and neon signs. Coach stood. "This is Piccadilly Circus. It's famous just because of how busy it is. It is said that a person who stays long enough in Piccadilly Circus will eventually bump into everyone they know. So girls, does Piccadilly Circus remind you of any place in New York City?"

"Times Square?" Shannon tried.

"Bingo!" Coach said.

Shannon looked down on sidewalks jammed with people. A huge store sign caught her eye.

Welcome to Hanley's, the world's largest toy store

Shannon pointed at the sign. "Coach, can we go?"

"No time," Coach said. "We need to get to Buckingham Palace."

"So, Coach, who lives at Buckingham Palace?" Haley asked.

"The royal family," Coach said. "The queen and some of her relatives."

"How big is it?" Haley followed.

"It has six hundred rooms," Coach explained. "There are fifty-two bedrooms, seventy-eight bathrooms, a cinema, and a pool."

"Why is it so big if only a few people live there?" Abby asked.

"They throw huge parties," Coach said. "Fifty thousand people go to events there every year. Four hundred people work there. Two workers do nothing but look after the three hundred clocks."

"What a waste of time," Abby cracked.

"Very clever, Abby," Coach replied.

"Why is the palace such a big deal?" Erin asked.

"It's a symbol of England," Coach answered. "The royal family invites world leaders to stay there. During other times, like ceremonies to honor soldiers killed in war, people rally around the palace. It gives them a sense of comfort."

"Kinda like a church?" Haley asked.

"Yeah, that's a good way to look at it," Coach said.

"Why are there so many guards?" Haley wondered.

"They protect the queen," Coach said. "When she is home, four foot guards stand at the front of the palace."

"Why do they wear those crazy hats?" Erin asked.

"Those hats are called busbies," Coach said. "They're made from the skin of Canadian brown bears, and they're eighteen inches tall."

"Wow," said Haley. "I wish I could wear one in goal."

"Why do the guards stand still?" Erin asked.

"They stand still for only ten minutes at a time," Coach explained. "Once in a while, each guard will march up and down in front of his box."

The bus pulled in front of the palace. A huge crowd had gathered in front of the guards. Haley took the 'whoopee' cushion out of her jacket pocket and slid it inside the back of her jeans. She nudged Shannon. "Come on, now's our chance." Shannon hesitated. "I'm not sure I can do this, Hale."

Haley grabbed Shannon's hand and tugged her along. The girls wriggled to the front of the crowd, their teammates trailing them. Haley eyed the guard. He stared straight ahead. His face looked like it was carved out of stone. Haley and Shannon walked up in front of him. Haley looked at Shannon. "Shan, my stomach hurts."

Shannon nodded. "You better sit down."

Haley dropped to the pavement. The air popped out of the cushion. It sounded like a gorilla had passed gas. The guard pressed his lips together. His shoulders started to shake. His mouth opened and his teeth showed. And then he burst into a full-throated roar. Haley and Shannon jumped in the air, their teammates howling in delight. Coach Wiffle just shook her head.

Minutes later, Shannon and her teammates boarded a bus. Out the window, Shannon saw a pack of girls in bright red jackets. One girl had long red hair. Shannon pressed her face closer to the window. *Chelsea Mills and the Wave.* Shannon closed her eyes. *Hope I see those girls again, on the other side of the field.*

CHAPTER 12

SHOWDOWN: SWARM VERSUS WAVE

WHEN THE SWARM TOOK THE field that afternoon against a team from Spain, Shannon had a plan. *I need to score early, before they start double-teaming me.* Five minutes in, Shannon stole a pass and carved a path around three defenders. From twenty yards, she lashed a hard strike that rattled the far post and caromed into the net. Ten minutes later, Shannon latched onto a loose ball and sprang into the box. When two foes closed in, she set up Abby for a tuck-in at the far post. Spain got one back on a corner kick to close the gap to 2-1 at the half.

Shannon saved her best for last. With ten minutes left, she curled a long free kick around the wall and high into the far corner pocket.

In the waning seconds, Shannon gathered a wayward pass in the circle and burst free up the right flank. As the center back neared, Shannon cut inside. Her eyes up at thirty yards, she saw the keeper creeping farther off her line. Shannon stubbed her boot under the ball and watched it rise. The keeper scrambled back, but she had too much ground to cover. The ball dropped behind her and tickled the net just under the bar. The Swarm won, 4-1. Shannon jogged off, her teammates showering her with hugs. *The teams here aren't very good, but who cares? At least I'm cranking in some goals.*

When the girls gathered that night for dinner at the hotel, Coach Wiffle shared good news. "Girls, we are tied at the top of our group. If we beat Ireland tomorrow morning, we get to play in the championship game on Monday."

The chant grew louder... "Swarm, Swarm, Swarm," until Coach stood and put up her hands.

After dinner, Haley and Shannon rode the lift up to their room. "Shan, this is one of the best days of my life," Haley said. "We won two games, and we cracked up a guard at Buckingham Palace."

Shannon smiled. "Hale, we scored four goals in both our games today, can you believe that? I mean, when was the last time we scored four goals? Wait, don't answer that."

"Shan, you scored five goals in two games today," Haley exclaimed. "Watching you own the field, it reminded me of how great you really are."

Shannon grinned. "Thanks, Hale. I haven't had that much fun in a long time."

Haley looked at her friend. "Shan, sometimes I wish you weren't so good."

"Hale, say what?"

"Here's what I mean, Shan. You're the best player on the Swarm, by a mile. That's good, but it's also bad. You get bottled up. And your teammates aren't good enough to take the pressure off you."

"I don't know, Hale."

"I do, I see it every game, Shan."

Shannon's thoughts wandered to the next day. "Can you believe we might play the Wave tomorrow?"

"It's gonna happen, Shan, I can feel it."

"You think they'd double team me?" Shannon asked.

"No way, Shan. They're the Wave, champions of the free world. They're too cool to double team anyone, even you."

"Hope you're right, Hale."

Haley fought off a yawn. "I'm beat, gonna turn in."

Shannon flopped on her bed, worn out from her full day. A morning match, lunch at the pub, a walk around Buckingham Palace, and an afternoon match. She got out a book and started to read. Two minutes later, the book slipped from her hand and tumbled to the floor.

The next morning, rain pelted the field as the Swarm lined up against the team from Ireland. Shannon scored twice to lead the Swarm to a 4-2 win. The girls had earned a spot in the final the next day. After the match, Coach called the team in. "Girls," she asked, "what have we learned in the last two days?"

"We're pretty good," Abby said.

"Yeah, we don't win many games in New Jersey," Montana followed, "but we can beat teams from all over Europe."

Coach nodded. "You *are* a good team. Back home, you happen to play in one of the toughest leagues in the world."

"Who do we play in the final tomorrow?" Shannon asked.

"Some team called the Wave," Coach said.

"How have they done here?" Olga asked.

"They won all their games," Coach said.

"What were the scores?" Olga asked.

"The games weren't that close."

"Scores?" Olga repeated.

"Seven-zero. Six-zero. Nine-one."

"That's great," Olga whined. "We fly to England just to get creamed by another team from New Jersey."

"That's a lousy attitude, Olga," Coach snapped.

Olga didn't flinch. "Face it Coach, we're doomed."

"I think we can win, Olga," Shannon said.

"You're the captain, you have to say that," Olga sassed.

"No, Olga, I said it because I believe it."

Olga smirked. "What makes you think we can win?"

"They'll be cocky," Shannon said. "We can outhustle them. If we play our best, I know we can do it."

"I'm with Shannon," Abby chimed in.

"Soccer's a crazy game. We get a good bounce or two, we can beat the Wave. We can show Chelsea Mills."

Haley stepped up. "Girls, remember what Chelsea did to us? Quit our team, tried to ruin us. Does that make you mad?"

"Makes me really steamed," Abby cracked. "Makes me want to beat her so bad."

Haley started another chant. "Crush Chelsea, Crush Chelsea, Crush Chelsea!" Even Olga joined in. The chant grew louder, until Coach put up her hand. "Girls, I love your enthusiasm, but let's get on the bus. I don't want the Ireland players to think we're rubbing it in."

Olga waved a hand. "Coach, after the season we've had, I don't feel bad rubbing it in."

Coach set her eyes on Olga. "How did you feel when the Cheetahs danced around the field after they beat us?"

"It hurt, Coach," Olga said. "But don't worry, we won't do it after we beat the Wave tomorrow."

"Olga, Olga, Olga!" the girls chanted. Olga blushed. That afternoon, they had lunch at The Lamb and the Flag pub, followed by visits to Trafalgar Square and Big Ben.

That night Shannon stirred under the covers, the questions piling up in her head. *Will Chelsea mark me? Will she try to hurt me? How good is she? Is she better than me?*

The last question caused Shannon to sit bolt upright. *No one outplays me, especially not the girl who tried to keep me off the Swarm, the girl who played dirty against me. Tomorrow, I'm taking Chelsea Mills to school.*

Shannon dropped back on her pillow. She closed her eyes and tried to remember all the goals she had scored in England. She remembered the first three, and the next thing she knew, she opened her eyes to the first light of a new day. Shannon rolled over. Haley was already on the floor, stretching her legs. "You sure can snore, Shan," Haley said. "Sounded like you were barking at the moon."

Shannon laughed. She pulled back the curtain, saw the sun rising in a cloudless sky. "Looks like a great day to play," Shannon said.

Haley stood. "I know you're gonna play great, Shan."

Shannon put up her hand, and Haley gave her five. "You and me both, Hale."

Later that morning, the team rode a bus to the field. The Wave players were already there, doing drills over half of the field. Shannon led her teammates on a trot around the other half. As she jogged through the circle, Shannon told herself not to look at the Wave players. Her eyes didn't listen. She saw Chelsea, but Chelsea paid no attention. *That's okay, I'll get her attention soon.*

Soon, Coach Wiffle called the Swarm in. "Girls, they're going to announce the starting lineups on the loud speaker," Coach said. "When your name is called, run out ten yards, turn, and wave to the crowd."

Shannon was the last player called. As she jogged out, her chest thumped. Her eyes wandered over to the Wave's bench. Coach Dash looked her way. He nodded and smiled. Shannon smiled back, but quickly squeezed her lips shut. *What are you doing, smiling at the enemy? Snap out of it!*

Shannon stayed on the pitch to meet the Wave captain. They shook hands and fell into a staring contest. The other girl looked away first.

Shannon lost the coin flip. "We'll take the ball," the girl said. Shannon trotted back to the huddle. As Coach gave a pep talk, Shannon hopped on her toes. *I am so pumped, blow the whistle!*

As the Wave prepared to kick off, Shannon locked eyes with the girl she would mark. *Number ten, long legs, about to live a nightmare.* The whistle blew. Number ten sprinted down the flank, and Chelsea floated a high ball toward the corner. Shannon beat number ten to the ball. She turned, slipped the ball between the girl's boots, and lofted a long ball ahead of Abby. As Abby collected and dribbled across the center stripe, Shannon drew a deep breath. *Time to test the stamina of number ten.*

Shannon broke into a sprint. Number ten tried to keep up, but Shannon had five yards on her as she glided through the circle. Still running at full tilt, Shannon watched Abby lead Montana toward the corner. Montana gathered the ball and saw Shannon making a beeline for the far post. Her cross flew high, the wind carrying it into Shannon's path. As Shannon prepared to leap, she saw the keeper running toward her. Shannon jumped and leaned her head in, just as the keeper punched at the ball.

Bonk! Shannon felt a thump on her forehead. Spilling to the ground, she didn't know if her head had met the ball, or the keeper's fist. She turned and saw the ball, in the back of the net. Swarm 1, Wave 0. "What a header!" Abby cried as she pulled Shannon to her feet.

As Shannon jogged back to her half, she could hear Chelsea talking to number ten. "I told you she was fast, Rachel. You can't let her get free."

The Wave kicked off. They swung the ball from the circle to the left side, around the back, and up to the right wing. Shannon's mouth fell open a bit. *Four one-touch passes. Wow, I wish we could do that.*

Chelsea bolted toward the corner, and the wing played the ball into her path. Chelsea ran it down and drilled a low cross along the eighteen. A Wave player beat Olga to it and cracked a shot that stung the bar and flew over.

Olga called in her backs. "We can't give them any room. They'll put the ball away like that," she said, snapping her fingers.

With only Rachel on her, Shannon took charge in the middle. She passed well and sprang off her feeds, often running onto return balls in the corners. But each time she crossed, a skilled Wave back line hammered the ball out.

When the Wave got the ball, they avoided Shannon. Their center back played the ball out wide, and they built their attack from the flanks. Chelsea and the Wave forwards shook free several times, but Haley made a series of acrobatic saves. She also got help from her best friends – the posts and the bar. Three times the Wave hit a post, and twice more they hit the bar. Their last shot off the bar was a thirty-yard rocket off Chelsea's boot. The ball bounced all the way out of the box. Shannon collected, cut past two players, and bolted into open space. Abby ran to her left, Montana to her right.

Crossing the stripe at midfield, Shannon floated the ball over the right back into the corner. Abby caught up and drove her right boot into the ball. Her cross was a gem, flying all the way to the far post. Montana ran on and headed the ball back toward the other post. Shannon's timing was perfect. She ran on and drove her left boot into the ball from ten yards. The keeper dove but the ball sizzled under her hands and snuck inside the far post. Swarm 2, Wave 0.

A minute later, the halftime whistle blew. The Wave players trudged off with heads down, chatter breaking out among them. The Swarm ran off, smiling and high-fiving as they met by the bench. Coach Wiffle beamed. "That was your best half ever!" She let her words hang in the air before she put up a forefinger. "But we must do one thing better."

"We gotta be quicker to the ball in the back," Haley shot in. "I feel like I'm at a firing range."

"Haley's right, we can't give them room to shoot," Coach said. "We've gotten away with it so far, but we won't the whole game."

Shannon raised her hand. "We need to keep passing the ball forward. If we just burp it out, we'll invite them back into the game."

Coach smiled. "Shan, I couldn't have said it better myself. Pass and move, girls."

At the other bench, Coach Dash tried to calm his team. Shannon cocked her ear in that direction. "Girls," Coach Dash said, "I know this is the first time we've been behind all season."

"We're not just behind, we're behind by two," one girl whined.

"I'm not worried," Coach Dash shot back.

"We're outplaying them. With a little luck, we'd have five or six goals."

Coach Dash paused for a bit. "We haven't double-teamed a player all year," he said. "But that number eleven, she's killing us. She's all over the field, and she never gets tired."

"I need help, Coach," Rachel said. "Like you said, that girl's fast, and she never stops."

Coach Dash looked at a defender, a blond girl named Mattie. "Mattie, you and Rachel will stay with number eleven, all over the field."

Chelsea spoke. "Be ready to run your tails off, girls. Shannon Swift will run until the final whistle. Trust me, I know."

The second half started like a different game. Shannon took a pass from Olga and spun into the circle, but Rachel and Mattie blocked her path. She tried to split them, but Mattie knocked the ball free. A Wave forward collected, beat Olga, and ripped a thunderous strike from thirty yards. Haley was caught flatfooted. She could only watch as the ball flew past her and cracked the post. This time, the post was not Haley's friend. The ball caromed into the goal, cutting the Swarm's lead in half.

Shannon ran back and draped her arms

around Olga and Haley. "Keep your heads up, girls. We're still ahead."

But Shannon no longer had room to roam. Wherever she went, Rachel and Mattie put the clamps on her. The Wave began to control midfield. They worked the ball to the front, where the Wave forwards unloaded on Haley. Haley parried several shots, but the Wave were relentless. With ten minutes to play, the ball rolled over the sideline near midfield. Shannon looked for her dad, but then caught herself. A bit later Chelsea stole a pass, fed a teammate, and took a return ball near the top of the box. Olga stepped up to challenge, but Chelsea faked left and cut free to the right. She hammered a low bolt that skipped past Haley into the far corner. Swarm 2, Wave 2.

Now it was like the Swarm was playing up a steep hill. The Wave won every free ball at midfield and kept pressing into the box. The Swarm backs would clear the ball, but not with any purpose. Haley was under constant attack. Finally, Shannon gave her keeper a break. She latched onto a stray pass and built speed through the circle. When two players neared, Shannon knifed between them. She dribbled around three more opponents and moved into shooting range. As she cocked her leg to shoot, Chelsea slid in. Chelsea got her boot on the ball and knocked Shannon to the ground. The ball squirted over the end line.

Chelsea stood first and offered her hand to Shannon. Shannon took it and Chelsea pulled her up. Their eyes met, but neither girl said a word. With three minutes left, the Wave earned a corner kick. The ball sailed to the back post, where Chelsea soared over Olga and headed it into the corner. Wave 3, Swarm 2. A minute later, Shannon pounced on a loose ball and made a long run down the flank. She crossed toward the back post, but the keeper snagged the ball and hurled it to Chelsea. Chelsea fed her left wing, who quickly swung a long ball across the pitch into open space. The right wing gathered on the run and dashed alone into the box. Haley came out, but the girl dribbled around her and tucked the ball into the goal.

A minute later the final whistle blew. Wave 4, Swarm 2. Shannon dropped to the ground and closed her eyes. When she opened them, she saw Chelsea's hand reaching toward her. Shannon took it and got to her feet. "Nice game,

Shannon," Chelsea said. "You're the best player we've faced all year."

Chelsea's words stunned Shannon. Finally, she said, "Uh, thanks, Chelsea, you played a really good game."

Coach Wiffle called in the girls. Haley was in tears. "I cost us the game," she whimpered.

Coach put an arm around her. "Shake it off, Haley. You played the game of your life."

"But I let in four goals in the second half."

"You kept us in the game, Hale," Shannon cut in. "Any other keeper, it would have been ten goals."

Coach put up a hand. "Girls, you made me proud, the way you hustled right up to the end. My word for the day is 'PRIVILEGE.' It means, 'great honor.' For me, it's been a privilege to be your coach this season. Come on, let's congratulate the Wave. "

At the end of the handshake line, Shannon came face to face with Coach Dash. "You played a phenomenal game, Shannon."

"Thanks, but it wasn't enough."

"Oh, it was more than enough for me," Coach Dash said. "You made this a close match, all by yourself."

"It was our team," Shannon answered. "We have some good players."

"True," Coach said, "but you're the engine."

Shannon smiled. Coach Dash looked around. The other players and coaches had moved out of earshot. "I saw three of your games this season," he went on.

"Did we win any?" Shannon asked.

"No, but it was never your fault," Coach Dash said. "You were always closely marked. Once, I saw a team put four players on you."

"It seemed to get worse with each game," Shannon said.

Coach looked into her eyes. "I still want you on the Wave, Shannon. I think you would be a perfect fit."

Shannon felt her heart beat faster. "You have a great midfield, Coach. I mean, where would I play?"

Coach Dash had a quick answer. "I'll put you wherever you want to play, Shannon. Look, I don't need an answer right now. Just think it over, that's all I ask."

Shannon looked at her boots. *I'm tired of being triple-teamed. Tired of Olga. Tired of losing.*

She looked up. "I've already thought about it, Coach. I'd love to join the Wave."

Coach Dash broke into a grin. "That's fantastic! You will love the girls, and I know you'll fit right in. I'll send you an email next week."

"Sounds good," Shannon said. She turned and jogged toward the bus. *My team just lost a game. But my heart is pounding like I just scored the winning goal.*

ACKNOWLEDGEMENTS

My parents, Bob and Dorothy Summers, took me to England as a young lad and introduced me to the greatest game on Earth. Laurie Summers, my kind and patient spouse, read many drafts and made each one better. My children, Kate, John, and Caroline, each shared helpful editorial insight. I received huge support from my brother Rob, my sister-in-law, Corie, and their two older daughters, Kaia Summers and Ruby Summers. Kaia and Ruby read early drafts, contributed thoughtful ideas, and even caught a few miscues. A big thanks to Glendon Haddix and his team at Streetlight Graphics.

ABOUT THE AUTHOR

Bill Summers is a soccer author, journalist, player, and coach. He is the author of the Shannon Swift Soccer Series, featuring *Magic Boots*, *Scuffed Boots*, and *Buffed Boots* (coming soon). Summers has also written the Max Miles Soccer Series, made up of *Clash of Cleats*, *Cracked Cleats*, and *Comeback Cleats* (coming soon). He is the author of the young-adult novel, *Red Card*. His book on coaching, *The Soccer Starter*, was published by McFarland & Company. As a parent, Summers coached boys' and girls' youth teams for over a decade. He was captain of the men's soccer team at Cornell University, where he earned his degree in Communication Arts. To learn more, visit www.billsummersbooks. com.

Coming soon...

BUFFED BOOTS

HERE'S A SNEAK PREVIEW

SHANNON SWIFT PRESSED HER HANDS on her shirt, but the noises kept coming. "You gotta pull over, Mom. It feels like fireworks are going off in my belly."

"The road's too narrow, Shan," her mom said. "Hang on, we're almost there."

Shannon was a half-mile from her first practice with her new soccer team, the Wave. She held her breath until her mom turned into Sunset Park and swung up to the portable bathroom. Shannon got out and hustled in. *This is crazy. How can I get sick when I haven't eaten all day?*

As she leaned over the sink, the fireworks

stopped. Shannon splashed water on her face, walked to the car, and got in.

"Feel better?" her mom asked.

"False alarm," Shannon said. "But I'm so nervous, Mom. I don't think I can do this."

Mrs. Swift put a hand on her shoulder. "What's troubling you, Shan?"

"Remember how Chelsea Mills treated me when I took her position on the Swarm? I can't go through that again."

"That was a long time ago, Shan. Besides, Chelsea was nice to you at that tournament in England. She said you were the best player the Wave faced last season."

"Okay, but what if I stink today?" Shannon countered. "I had mono for most of the summer, hardly touched a ball."

"Coach Dash knows that," her mom said. "He'll give you time to get your game back."

"He better."

Mrs. Swift saw a few girls warming up on the field. "Practice is about to start, you need to go. You want me to stay for a while?"

Shannon swallowed over the knot in her throat. "I'll be okay." She got out and jogged off, her red ponytail bobbing on her back. Shannon was twenty miles from home, about to take the field with the best under-thirteen academy team in New Jersey. Jack Dash had recruited her at the end of last season, for the second time. This time, Shannon decided she'd had enough of being triple-teamed. She left her town travel team, the Swarm, and joined the Wave.

But Shannon knew only one girl on the Wave. Chelsea Mills. They had a history – a nasty one. First, Shannon took Chelsea's position on the Swarm. Chelsea quit and joined the Swarm's rival, the Monsoon. Chelsea played dirty against Shannon and taunted her in school. The first time Coach Dash asked Shannon to join the Wave, she decided to stay on the Swarm. Instead, Coach Dash had picked Chelsea to join the Wave.

Sure, Chelsea was kind to Shannon when the Wave played the Swarm in England three months earlier. But Shannon still didn't trust her. And now Shannon was about to take Chelsea's position, for the second time, on a second team. As Shannon neared the field, she looked back and saw her mom pull out. The knot in her throat swelled. *This could be the worst two hours of my life.*

Shannon jogged toward four girls passing a ball in a square. The one farthest away wore a ball cap. As Shannon got closer, she noticed the hair under the cap. Hair the same color as hers, bunched in a ponytail, just like hers. "Shannon!" Chelsea called out. She jogged over and wrapped Shannon in a hug. Shannon snapped out of her shock and hugged back. Chelsea nodded to a spot away from the other girls, and Shannon followed.

"Remember how I was a kinda mean on the Swarm?" Chelsea asked.

"Uh, kinda."

Chelsea snorted. "I've changed. Coach Dash has taught me how to be a good teammate. You and me, we're gonna have a blast playing together."

"Sounds good." Shannon walked over and put her bag by the bench. *Wow, I didn't expect that.*

Coach Dash blew his whistle and sixteen girls gathered. Coach waved Shannon forward, and she stepped up. "Girls, let's give a warm welcome to your new teammate, Shannon Swift." The girls burst into a chant. "Shannon, Shannon, Shannon!" Coach Dash draped an arm around her. "Shannon will be a wonderful addition to our midfield. I know you remember her from our tournament in England. She scored two goals against us in the first half."

"Yeah, and then we shut her down," snapped Molly Horn, the center back. Shannon glanced at Molly, who glared back.

Chelsea broke the silence. "Come on, Molly, we had to put two players on her. Shannon's crazy good, we all know it."

Shannon blushed. *Did Chelsea just call me, 'crazy good'? Did she have a brain transplant?*